For my children,
Who could make a dad's life more relaxing
by being a little more boring at times . . .
—B. S.

To my children,
Who fill the boring days with wonder, humor,
and imagination. I love you so much.
—K. K.

Published by Roaring Brook Press
Roaring Brook Press is a division of Holtzbrinck Publishing Holdings Limited Partnership
120 Broadway, New York, NY 10271 • mackids.com

Our books may be purchased in bulk for promotional, educational, or business use.
Please contact your local bookseller or the Macmillan Corporate and Premium Sales Department
at (800) 221-7945 ext. 5442 or by email at MacmillanSpecialMarkets@macmillan.com.

Library of Congress Cataloging-in-Publication Data is available.

First edition, 2024
Book design by Sharismar Rodriguez
The art was created in pen and ink on paper, with color digitally added using Photoshop.
Special thanks to color flatters Audra Furuichi and Erik Scheel.
Printed in the United States of America by Sheridan, Brainerd, Minnesota

ISBN 978-1-250-84366-1
10 9 8 7 6 5 4 3 2 1

WORDS BY
BRANDON SANDERSON

THE MOST BORING BOOK EVER

PICTURES BY
KAZU KIBUISHI

ROARING BROOK PRESS | New York

A boy sat in a chair.

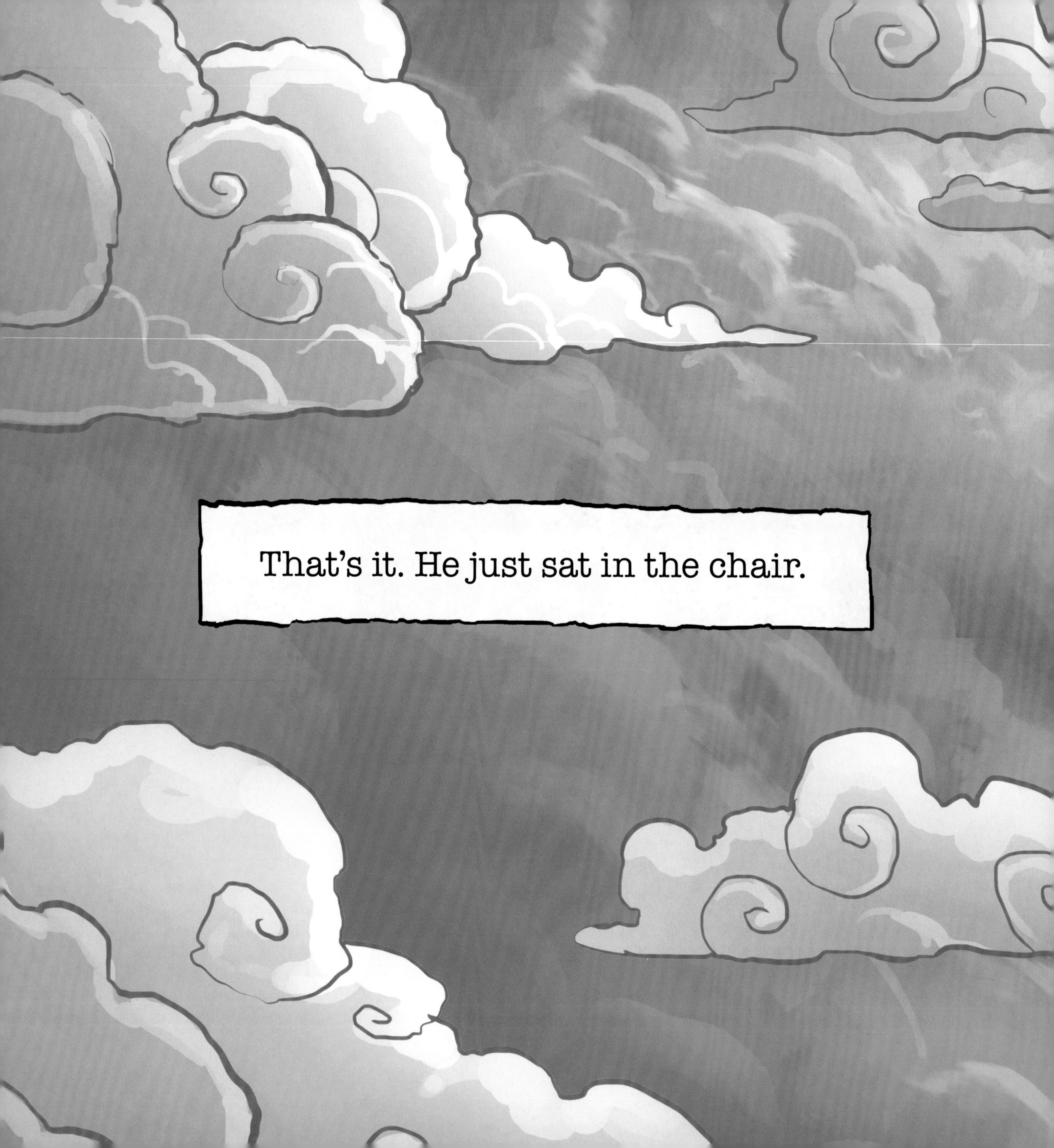
That’s it. He just sat in the chair.

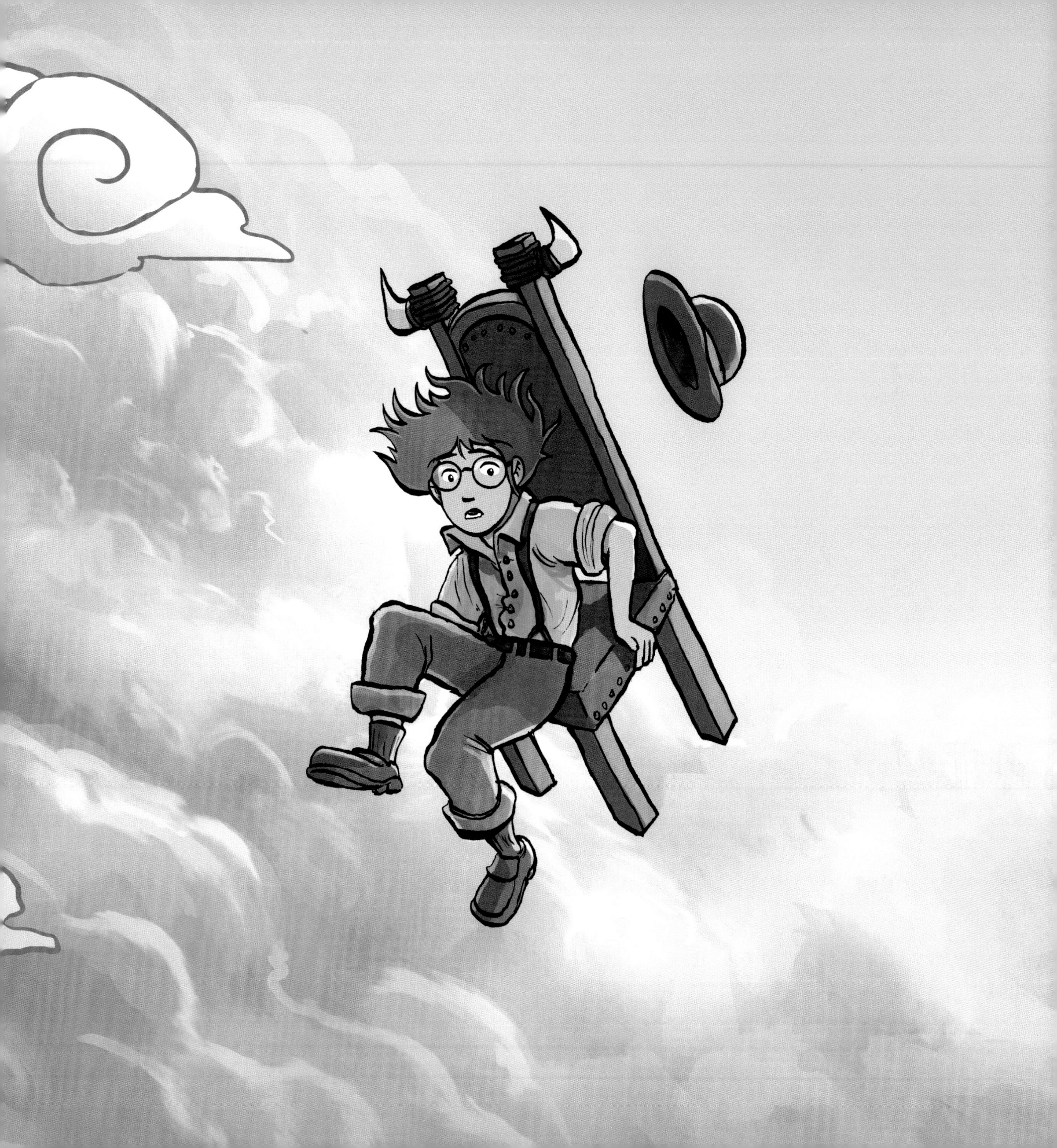

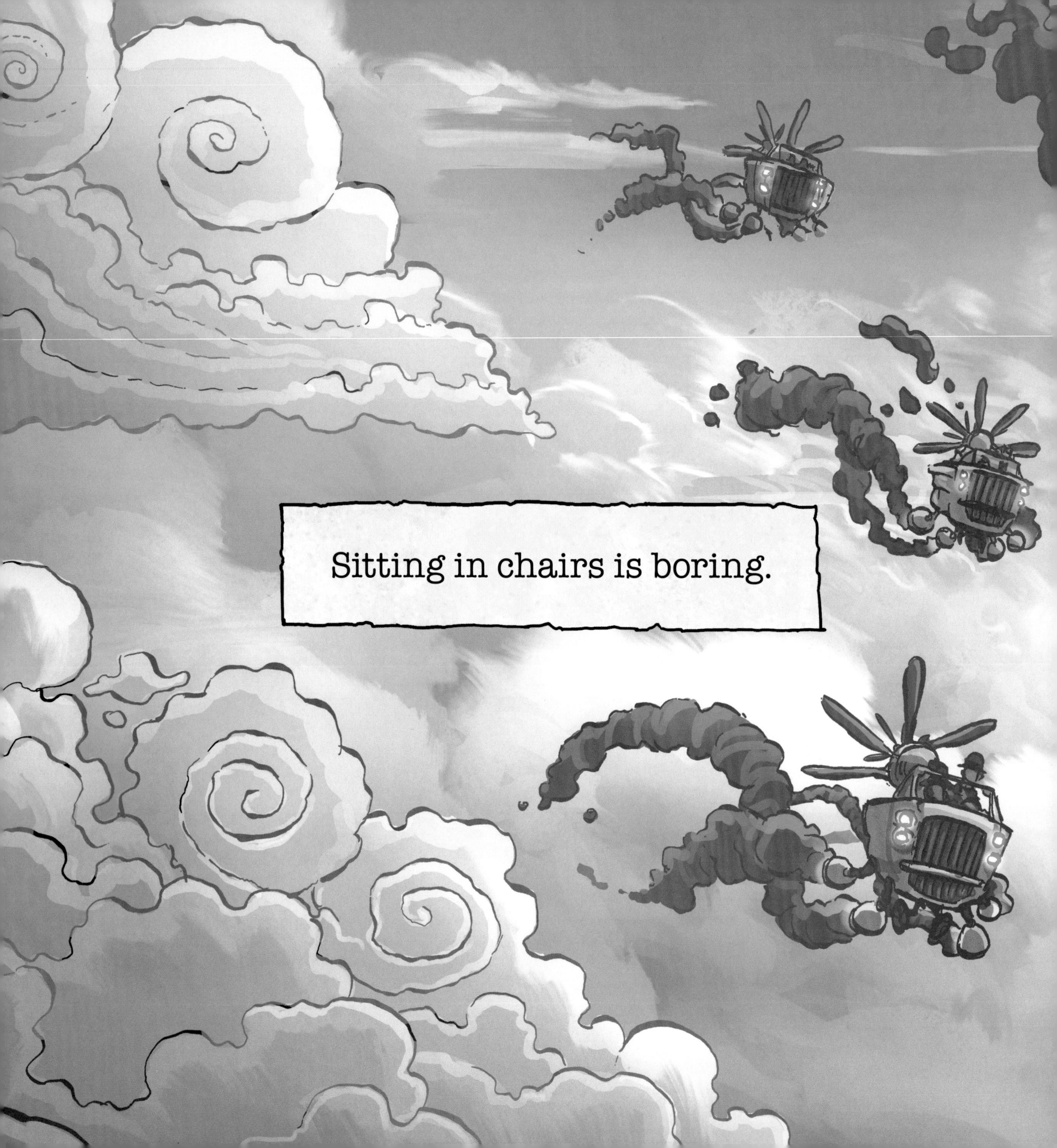
Sitting in chairs is boring.

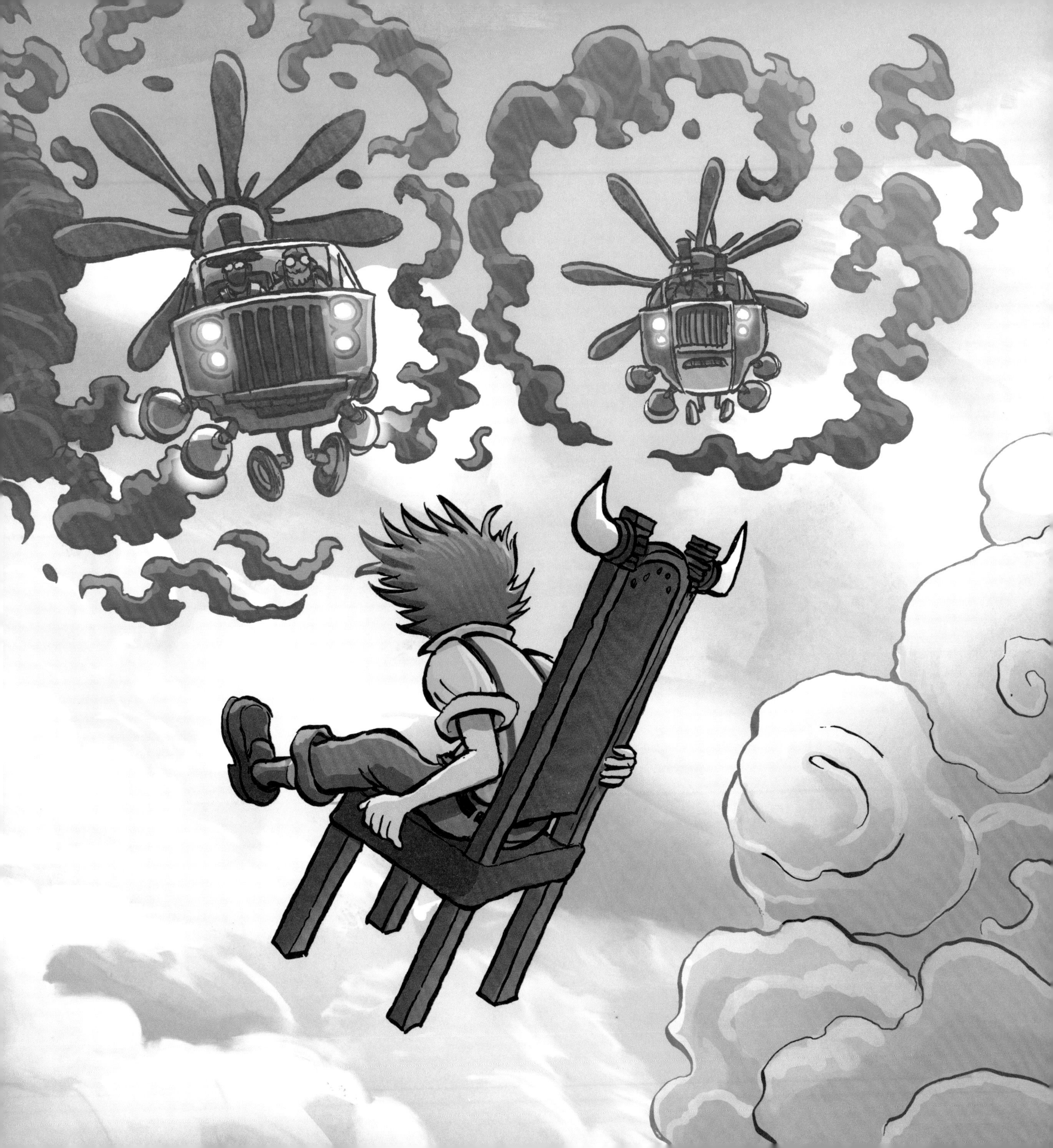

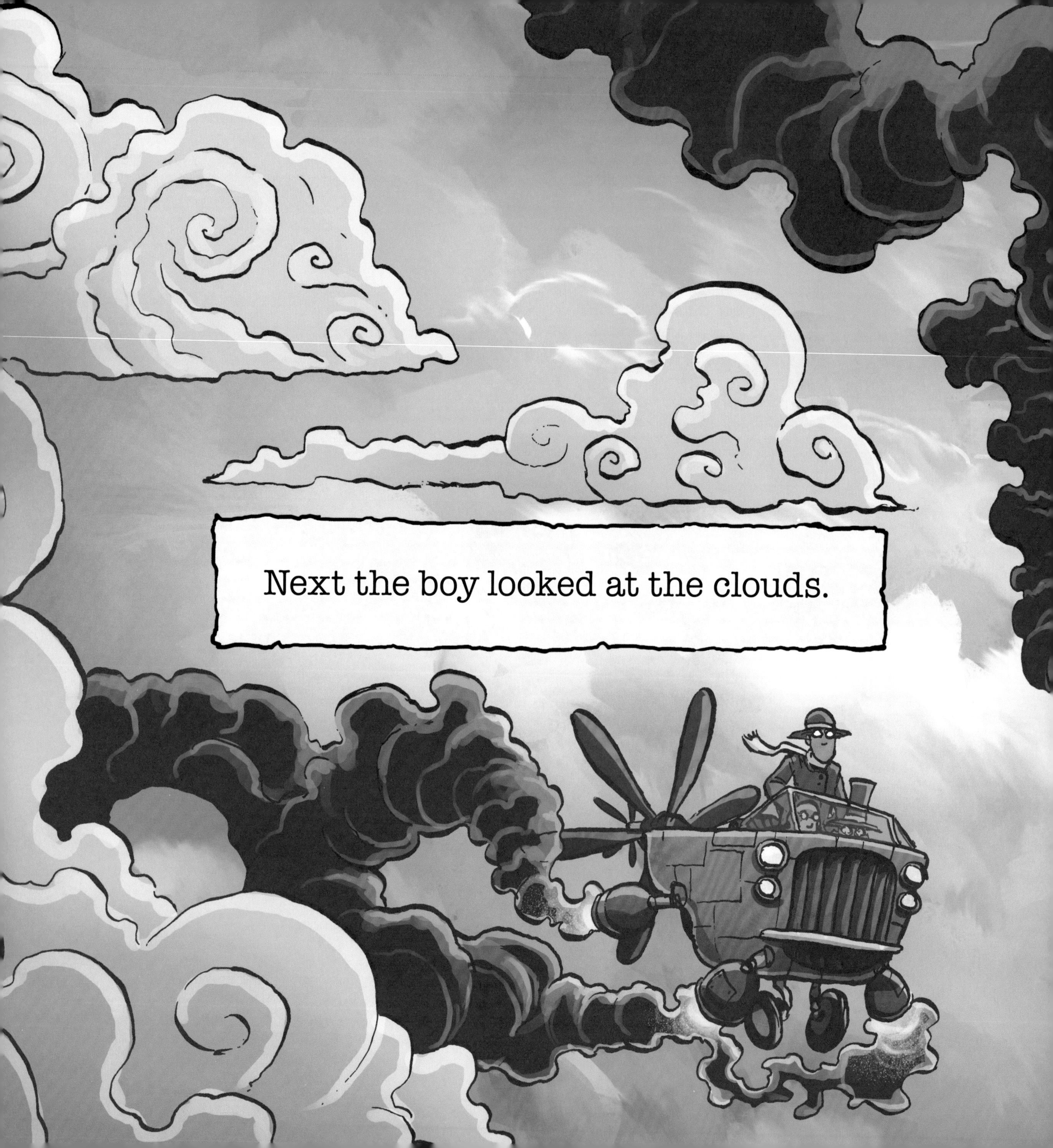

Next the boy looked at the clouds.

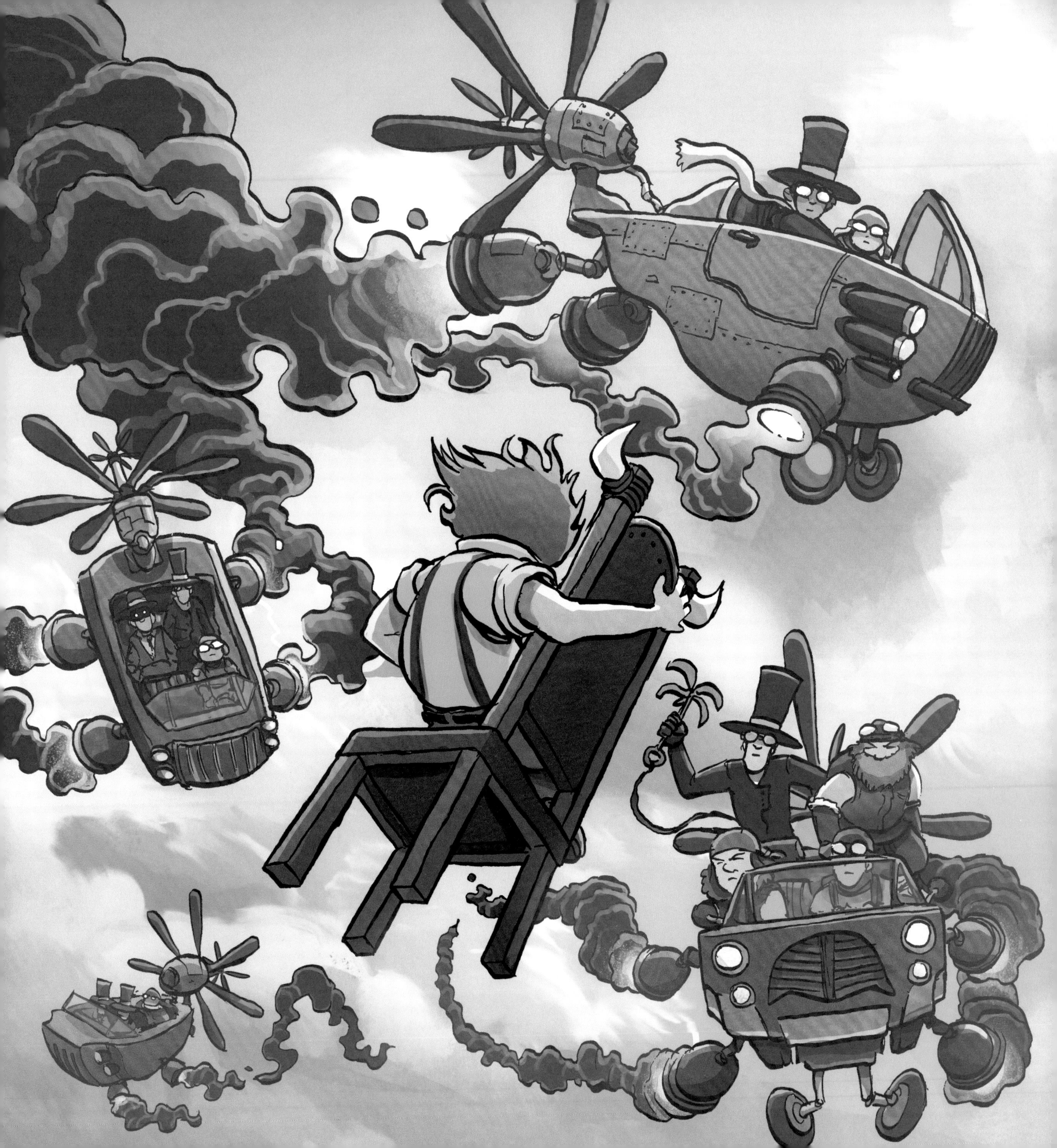

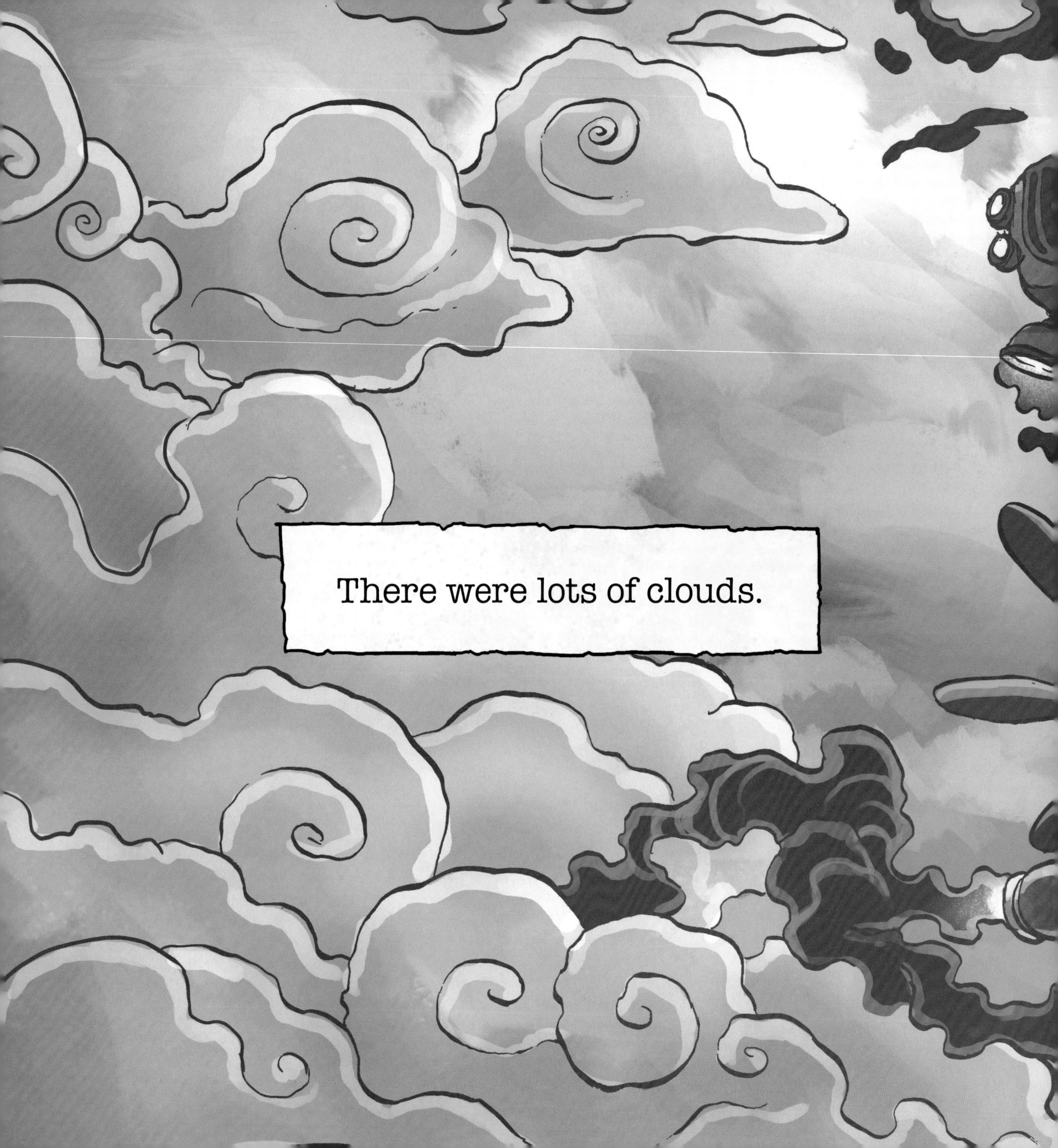
There were lots of clouds.

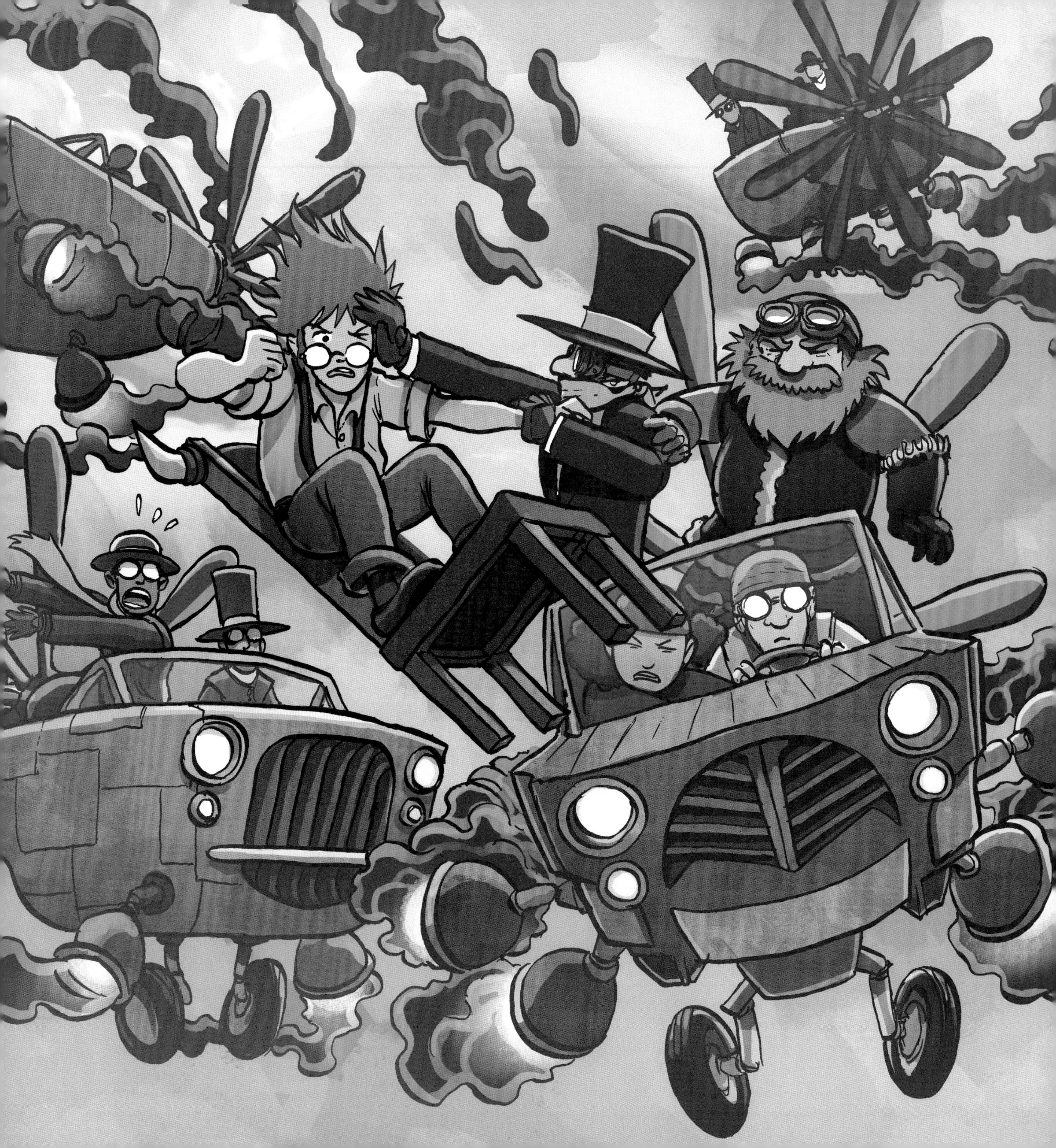

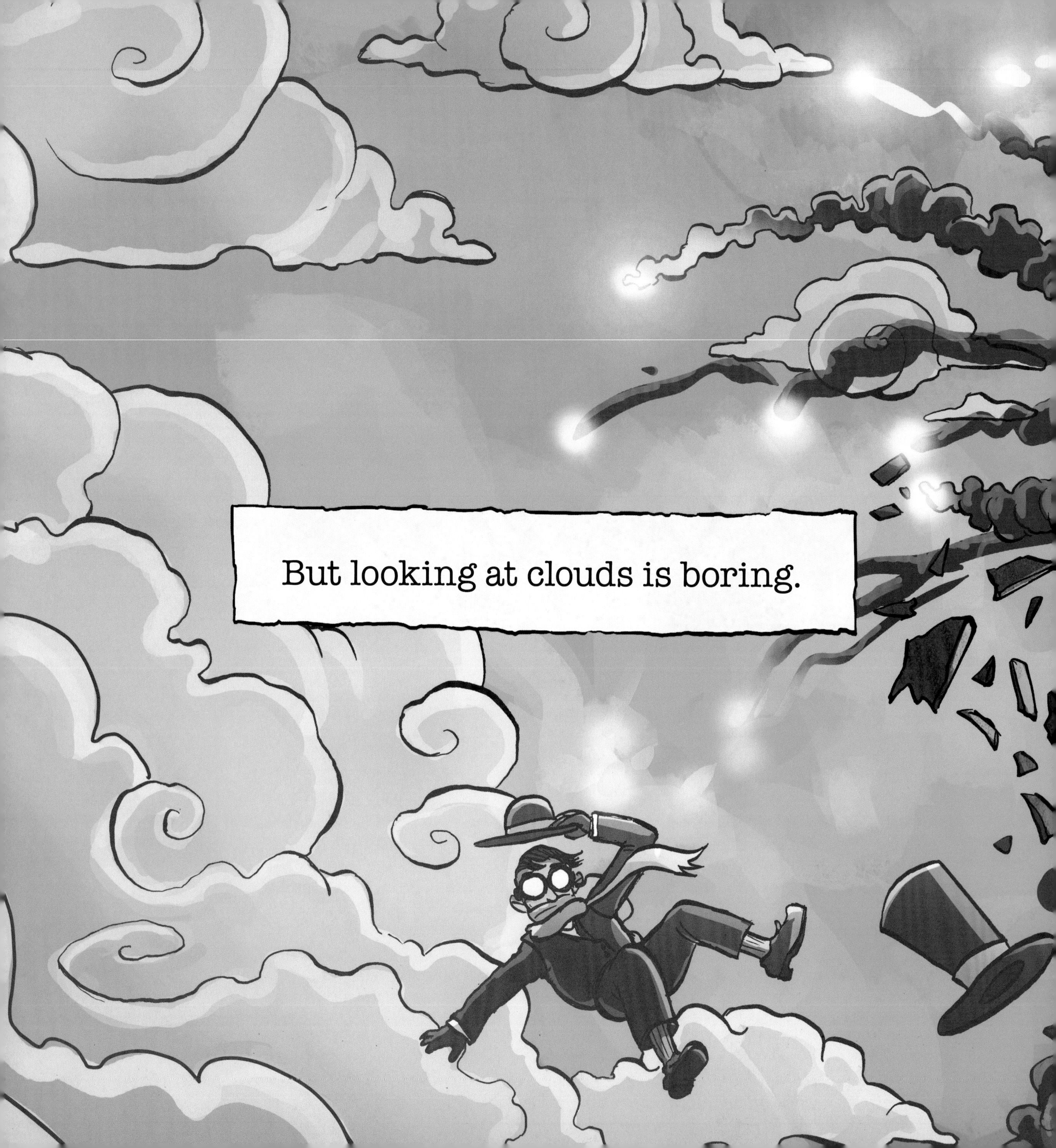
But looking at clouds is boring.

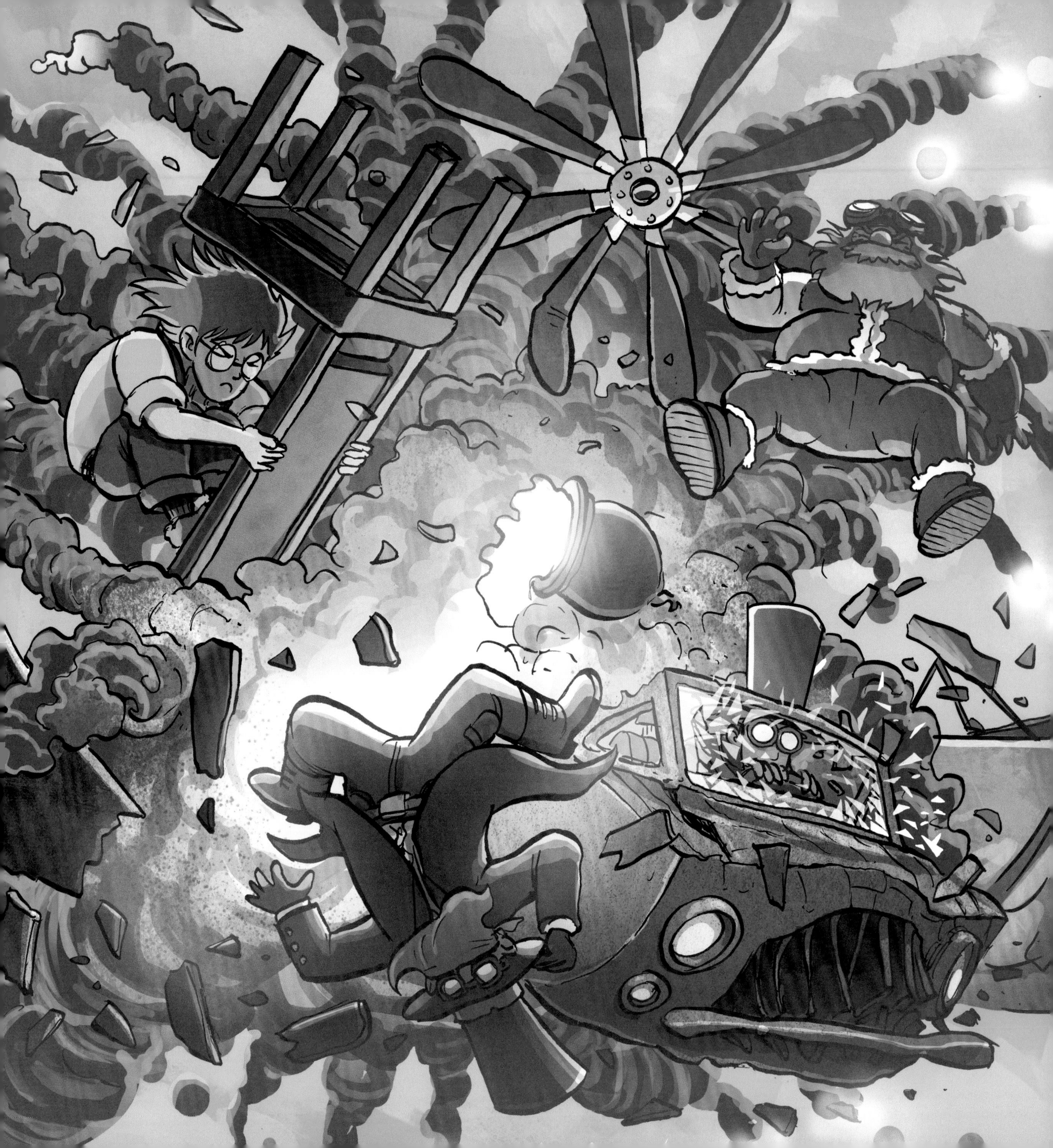

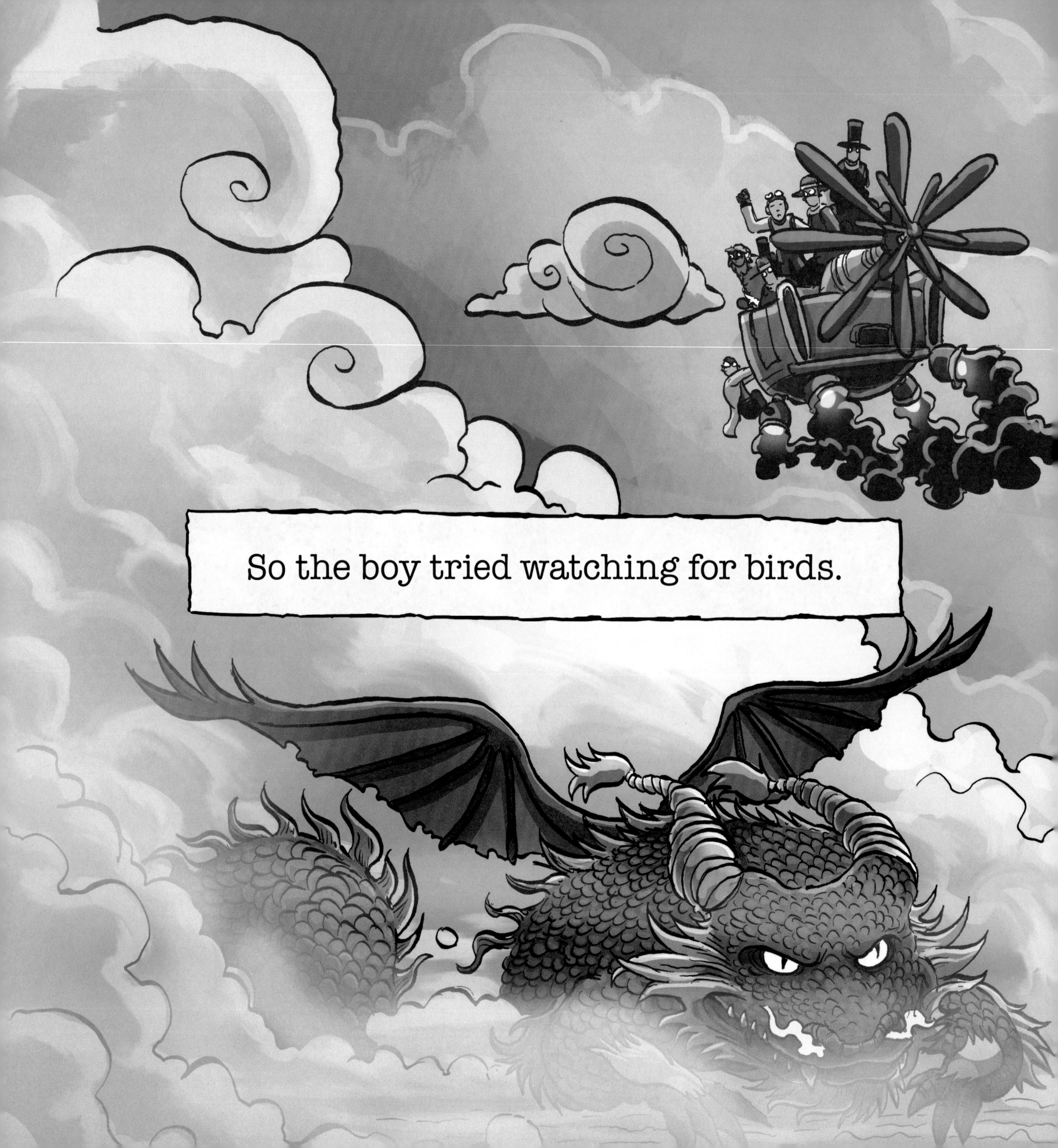
So the boy tried watching for birds.

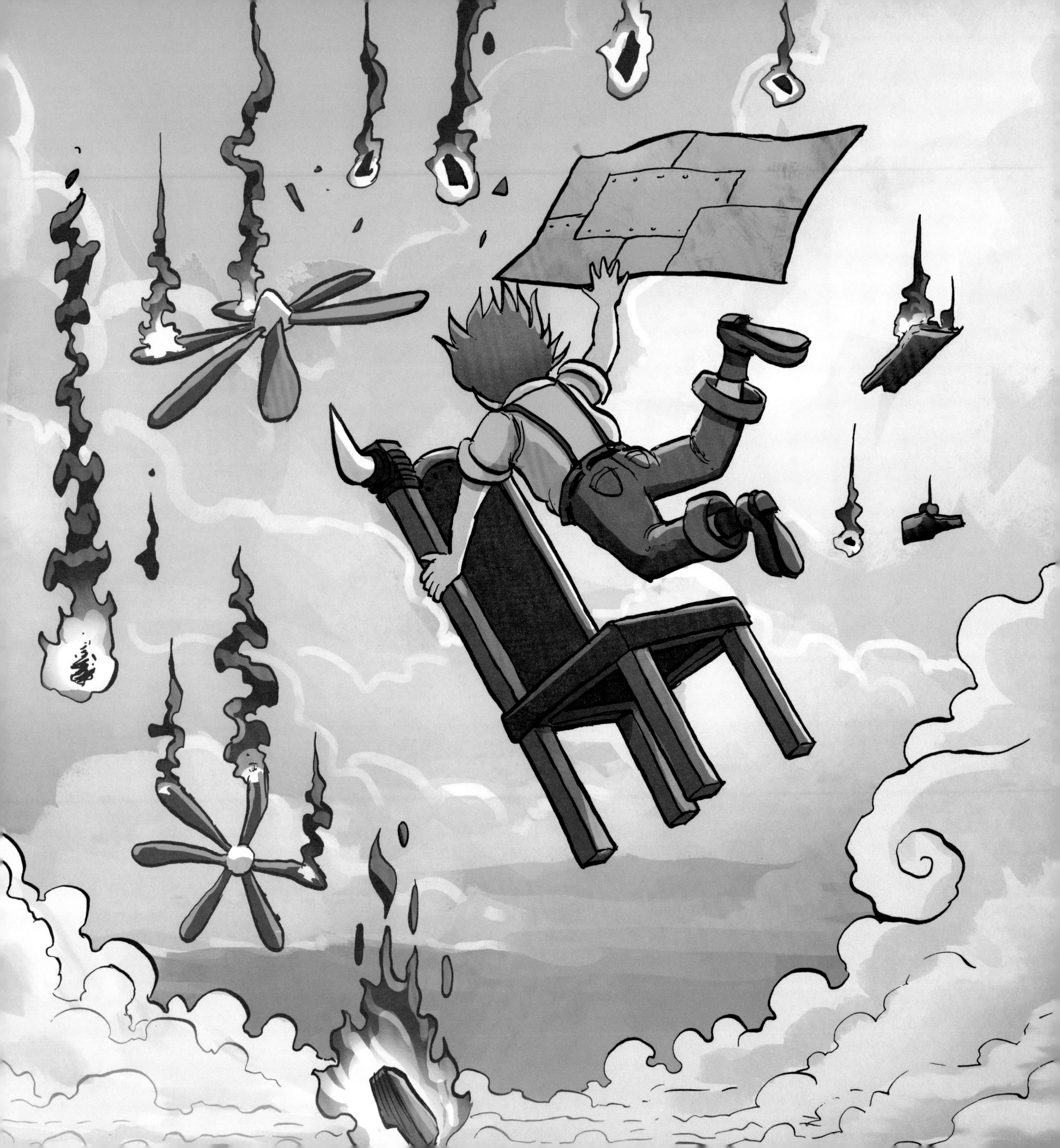

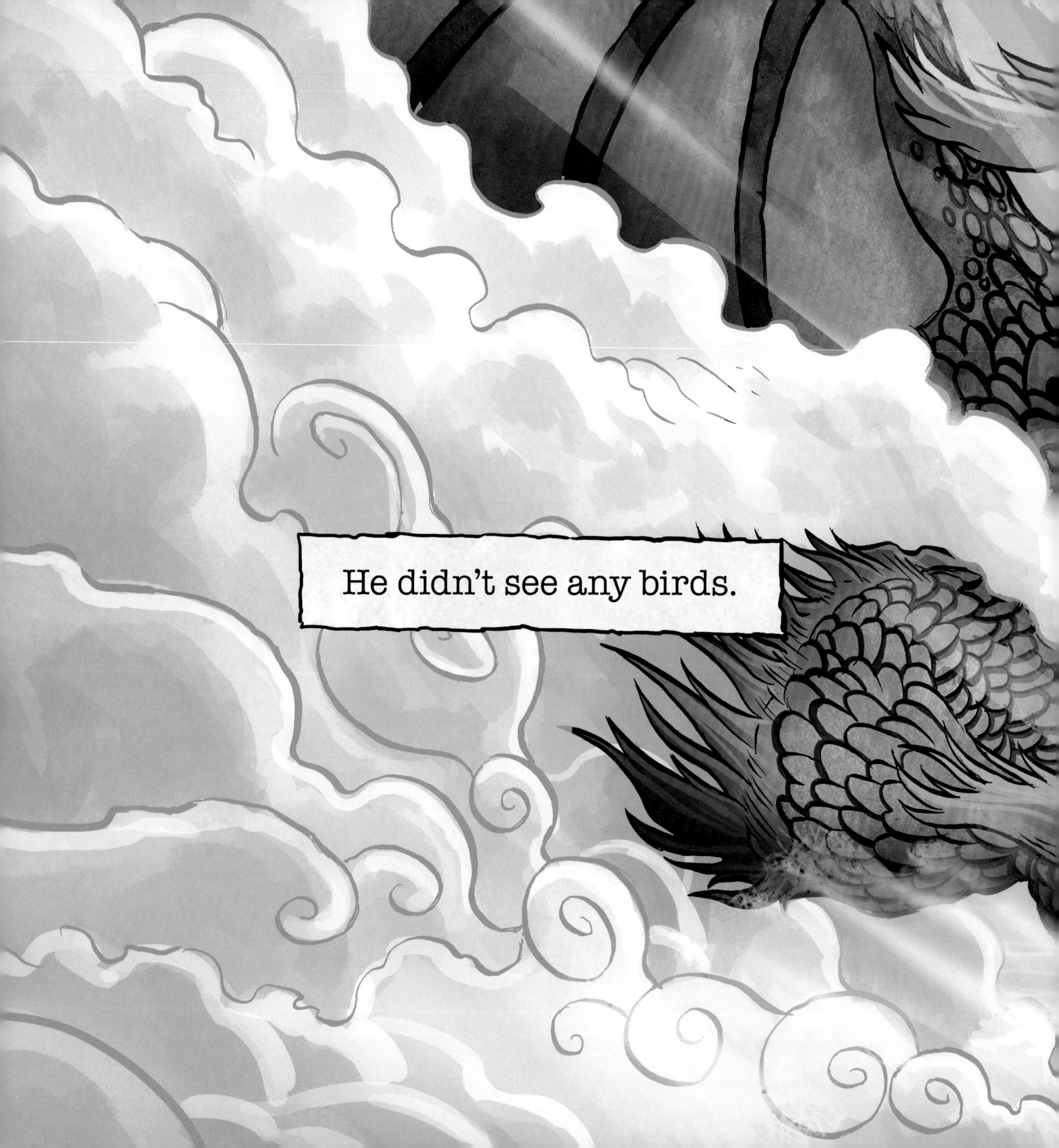
He didn’t see any birds.

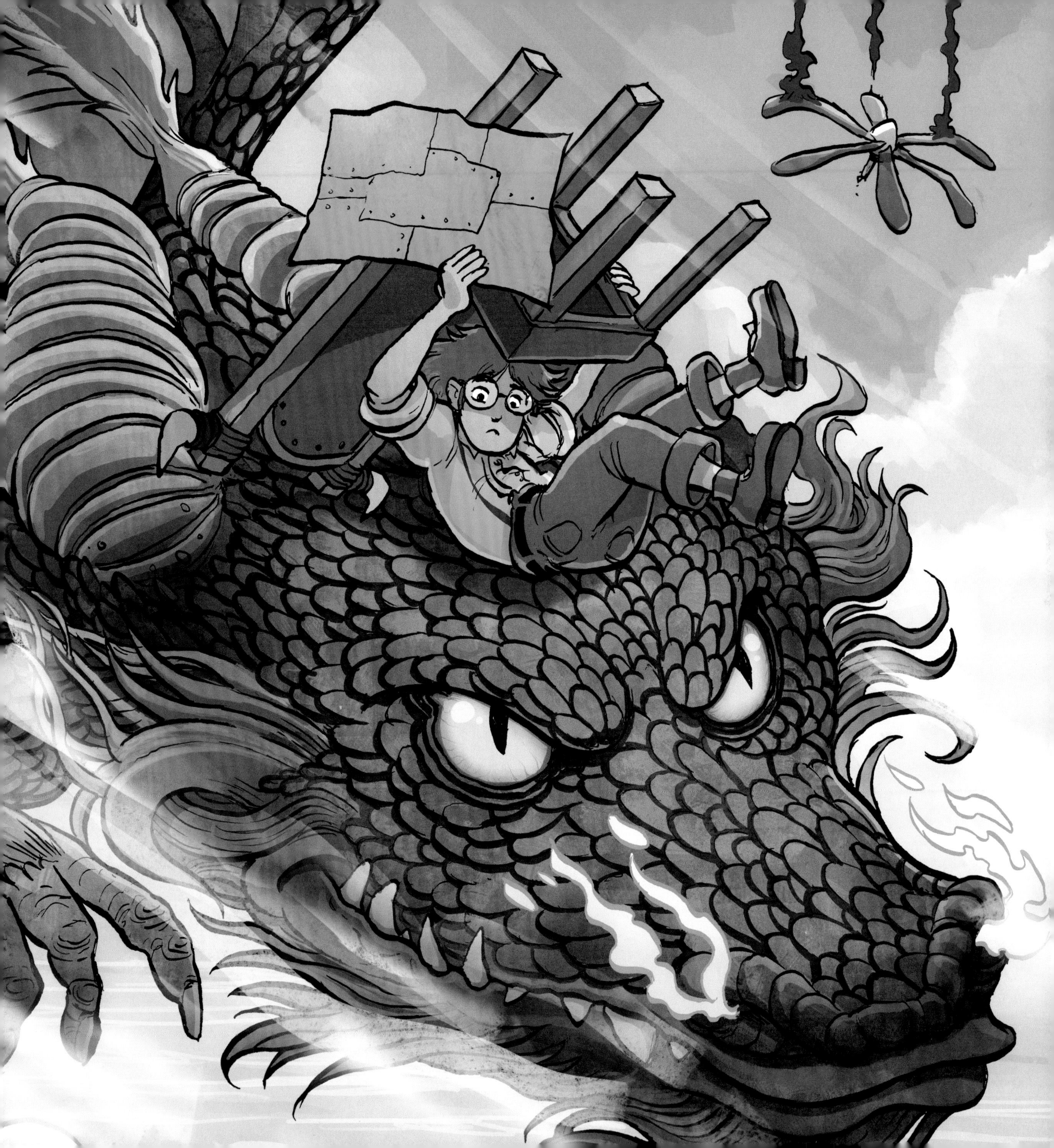

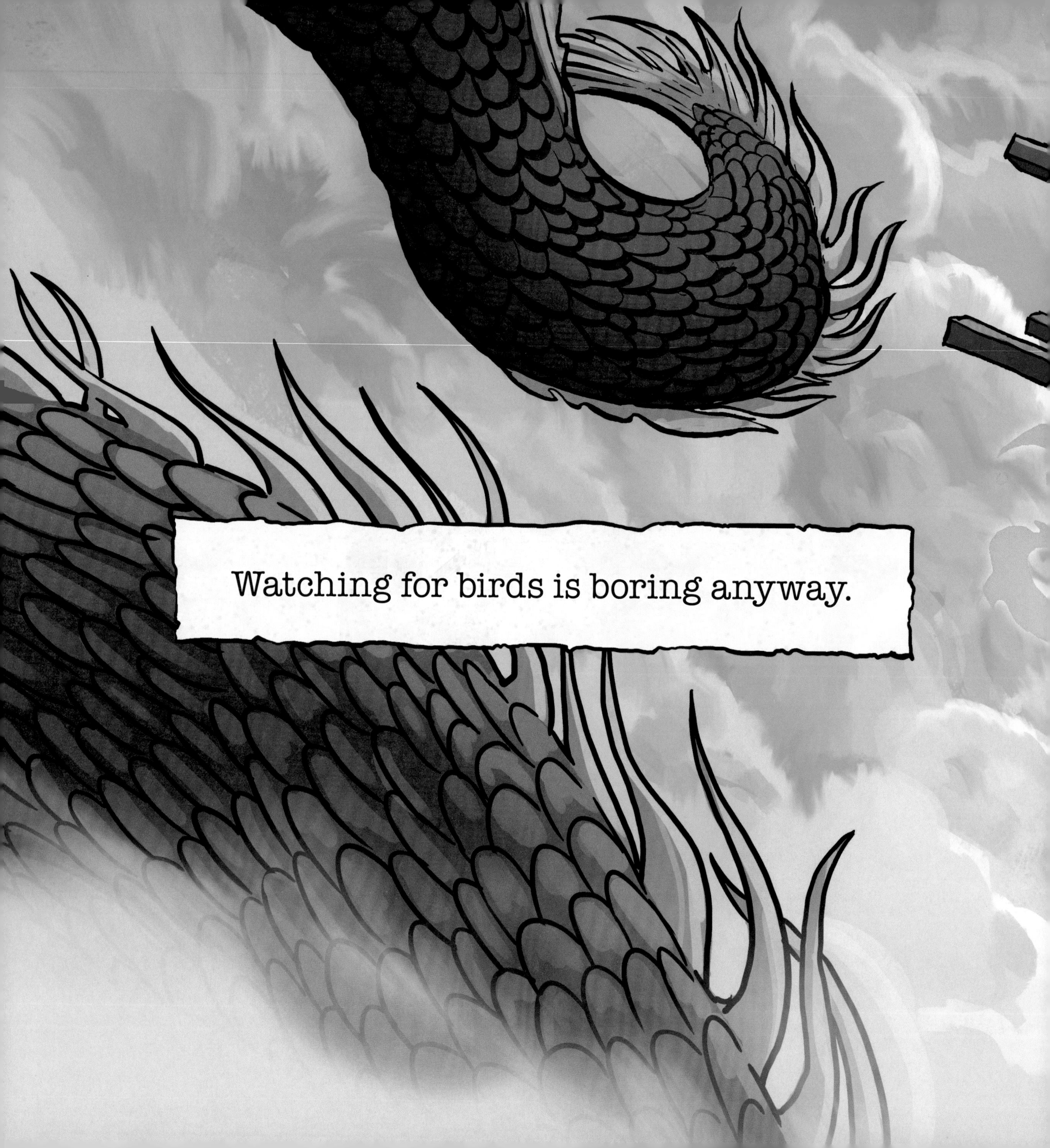
Watching for birds is boring anyway.

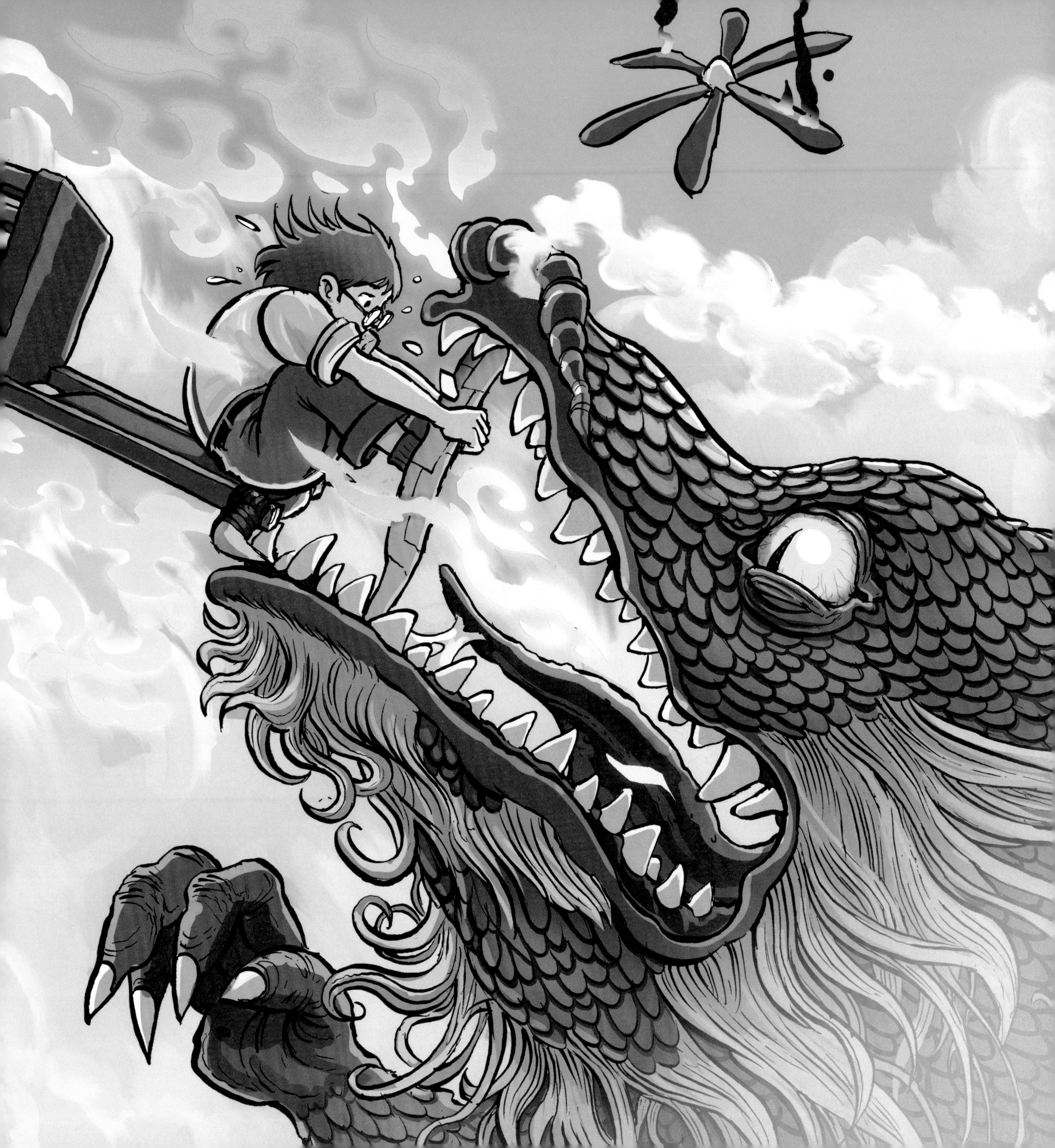

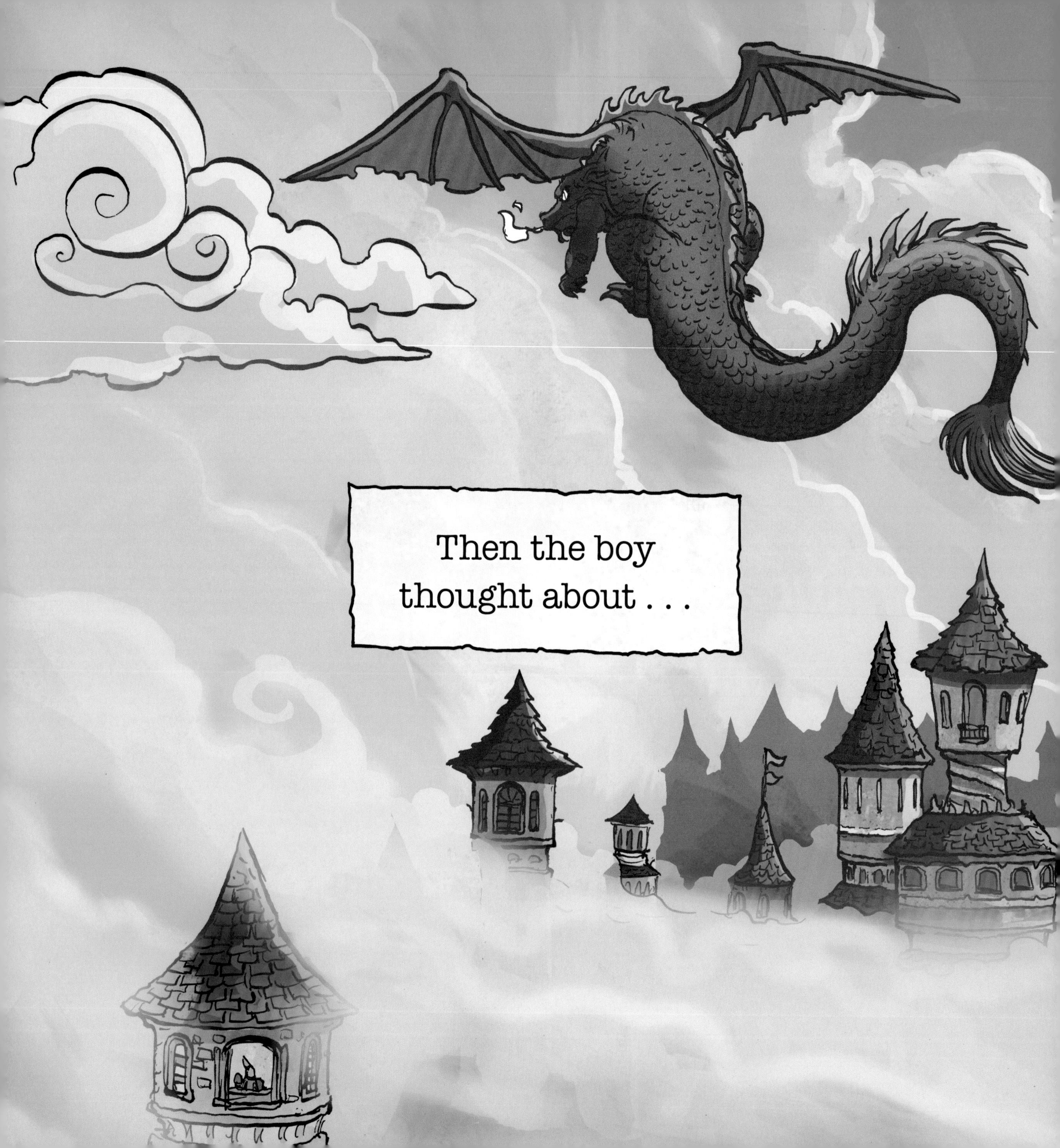
Then the boy thought about . . .

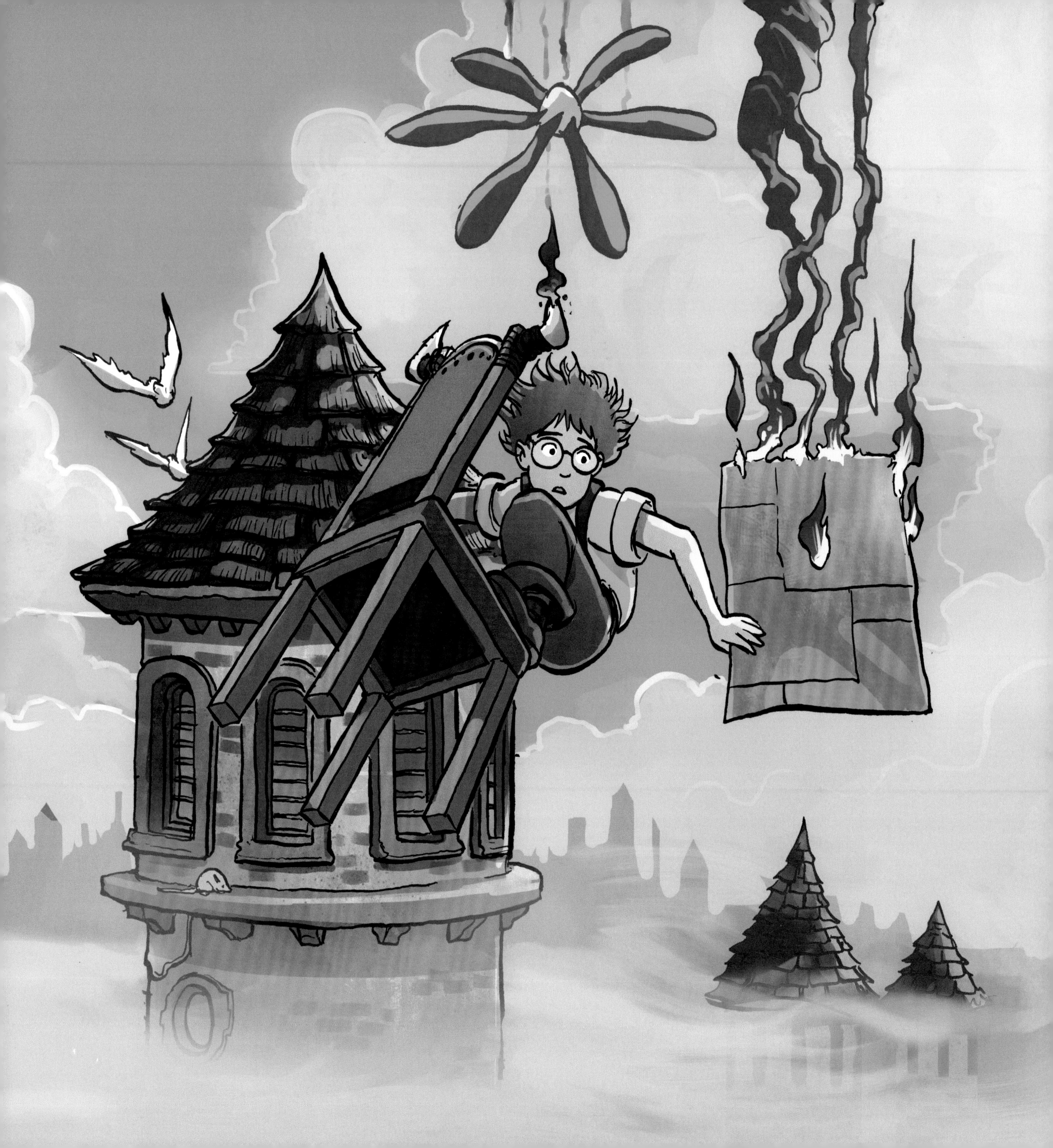

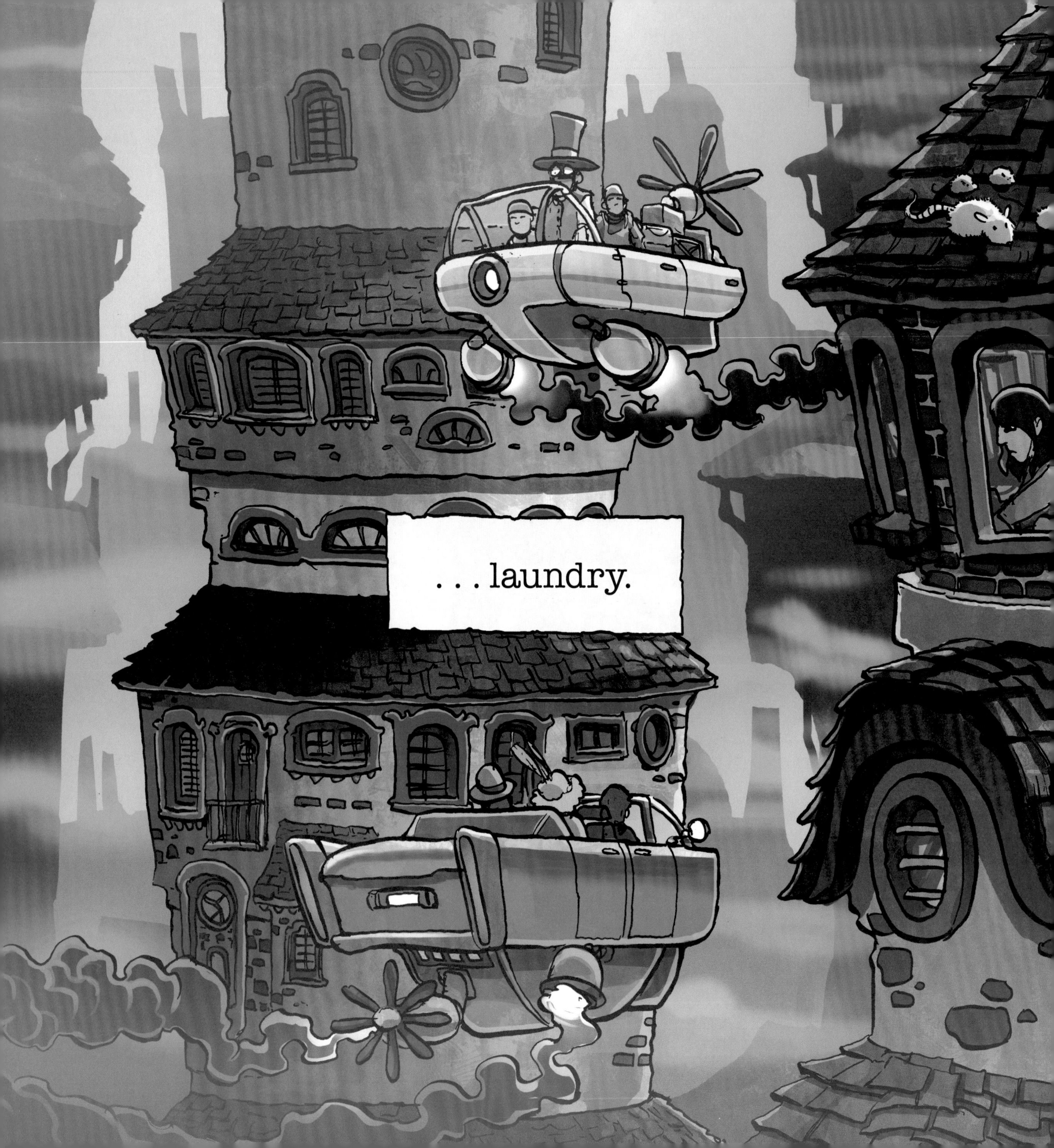
. . . laundry.

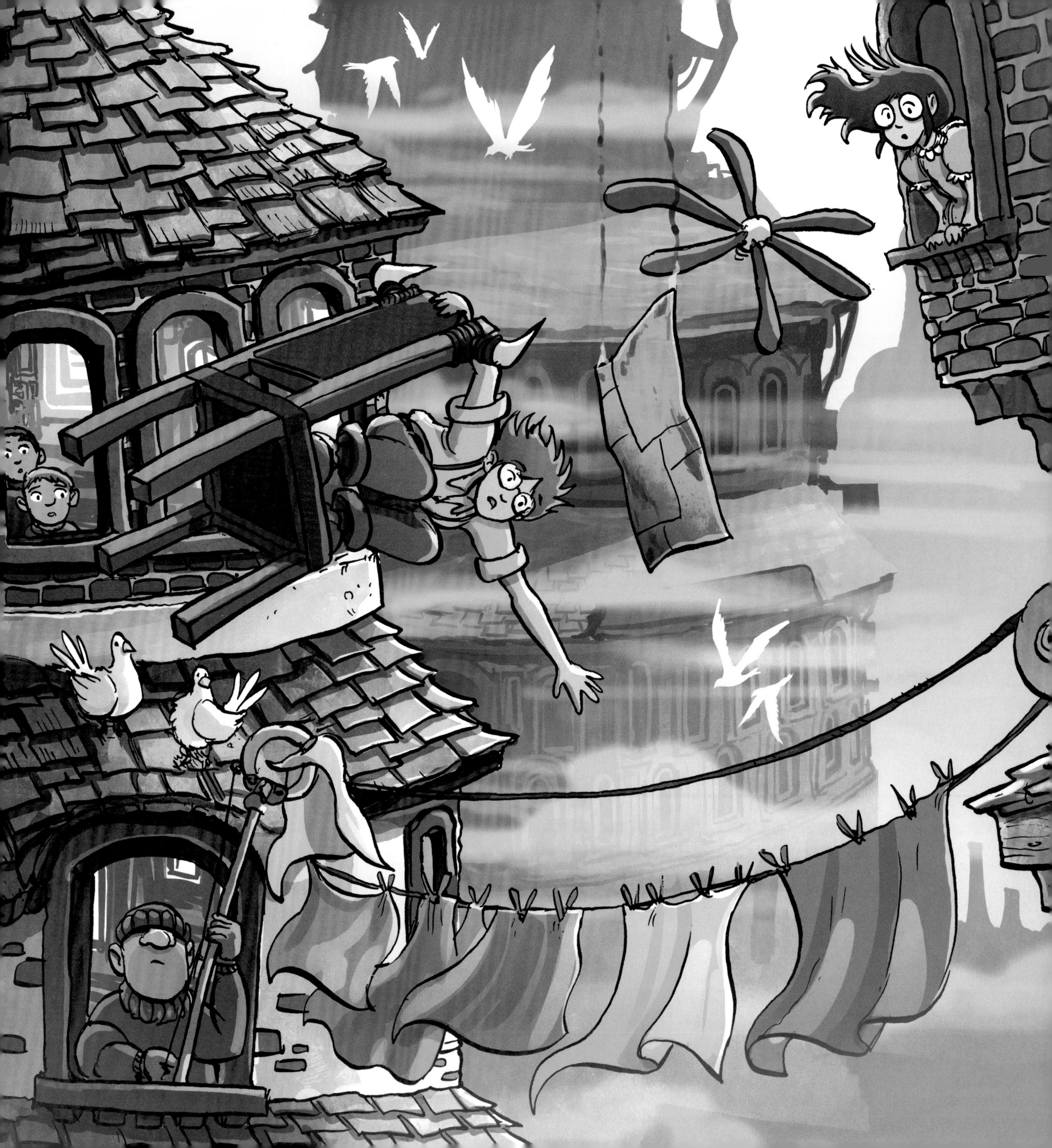

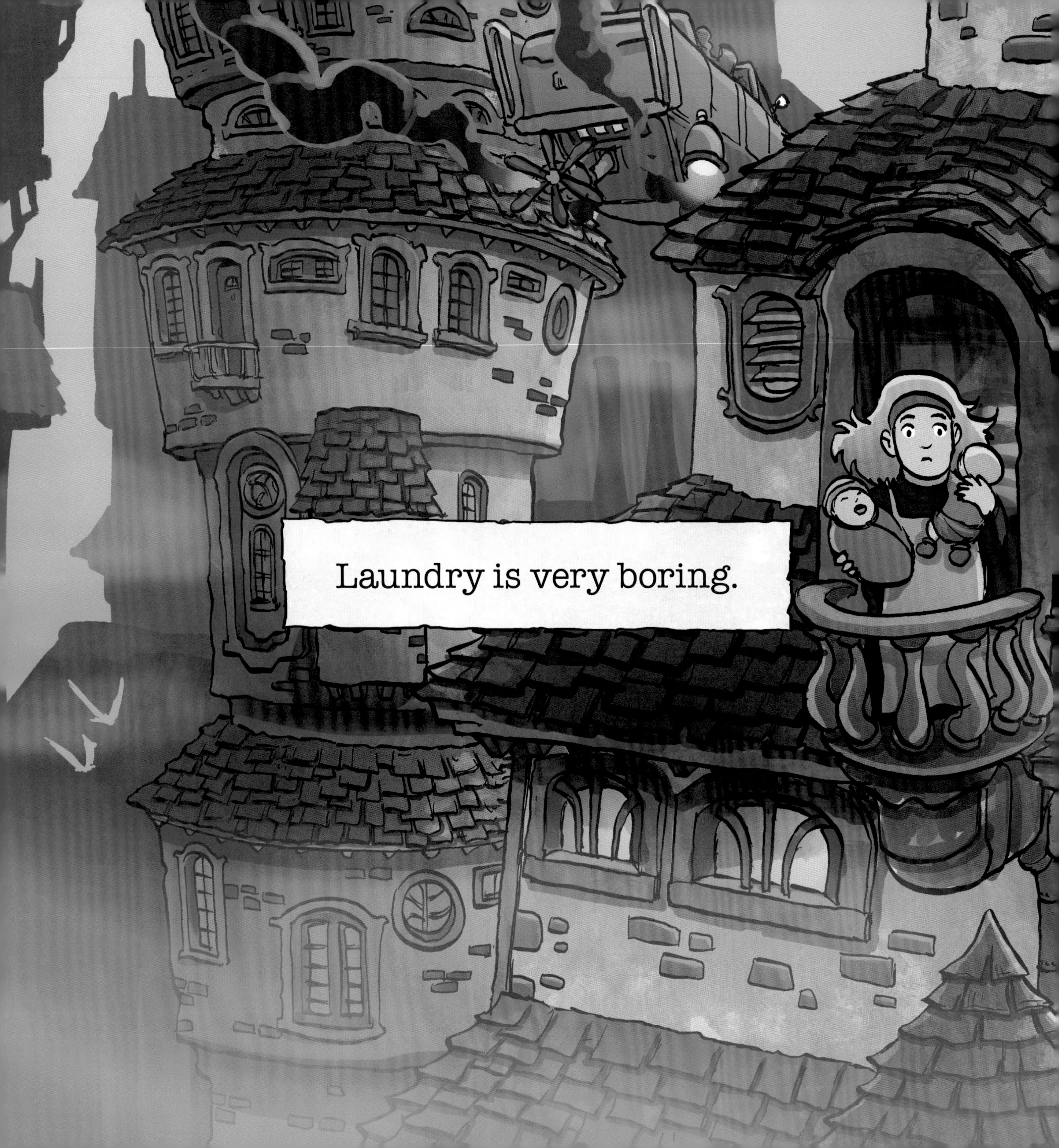
Laundry is very boring.

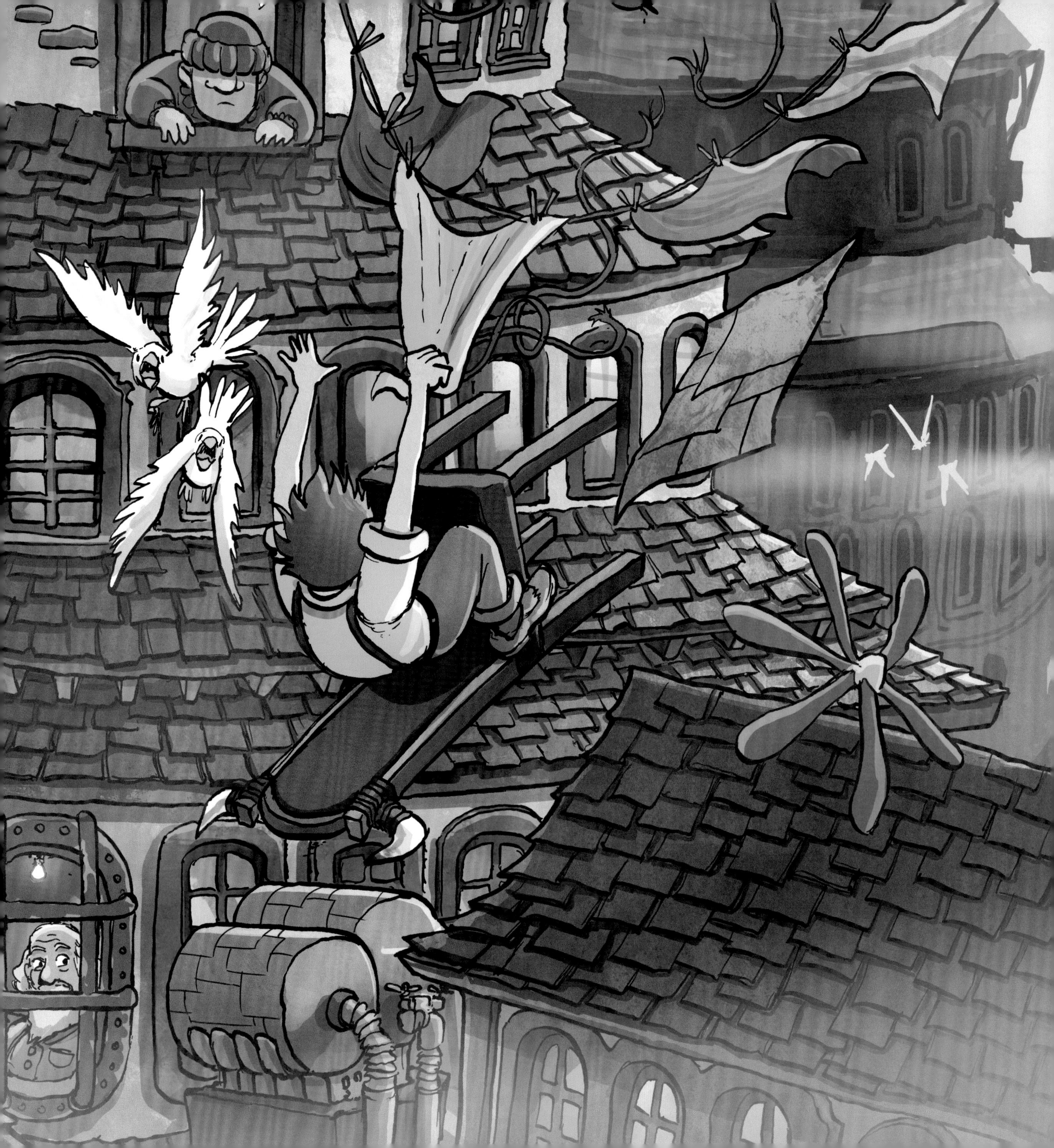

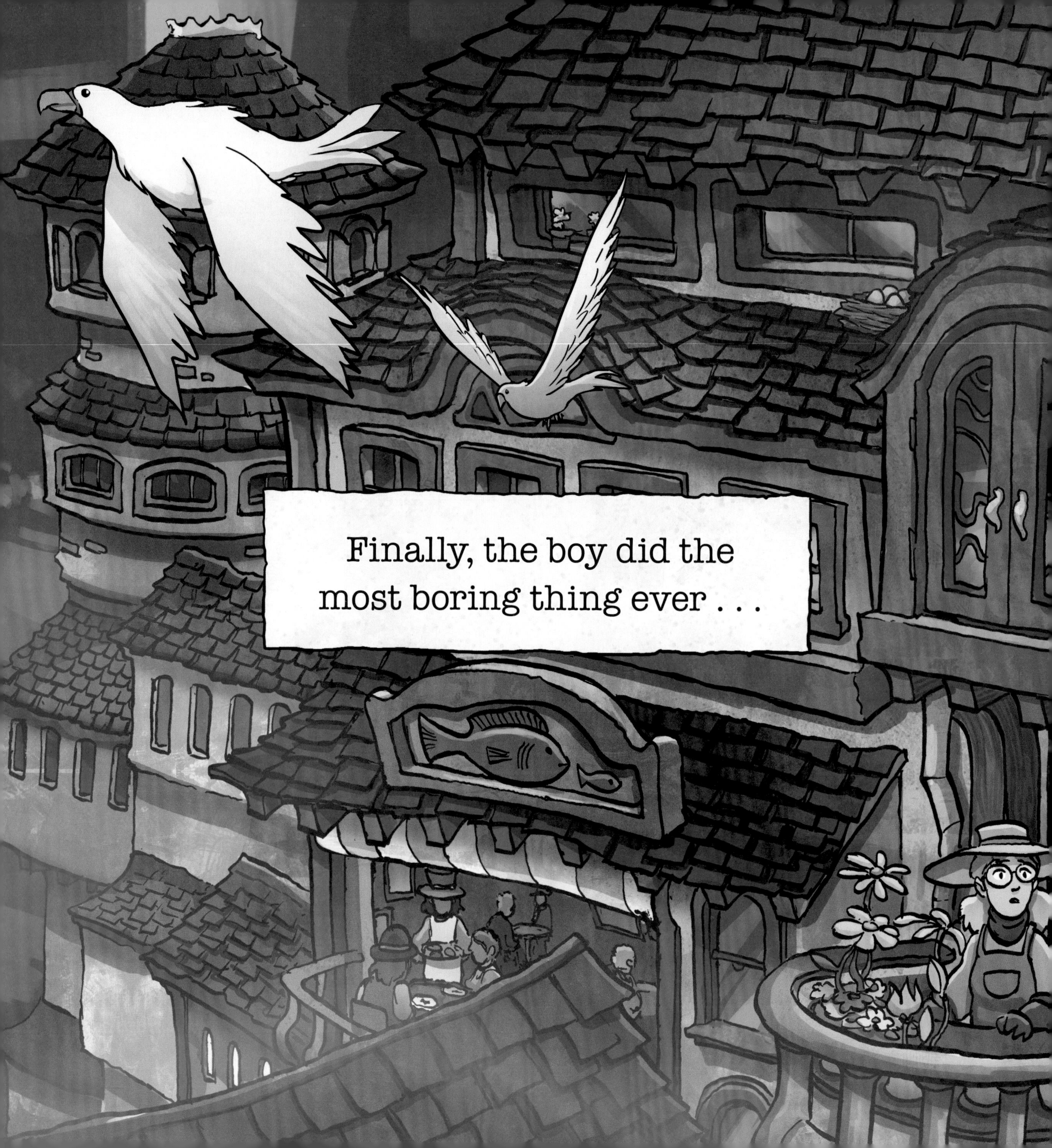
Finally, the boy did the most boring thing ever . . .

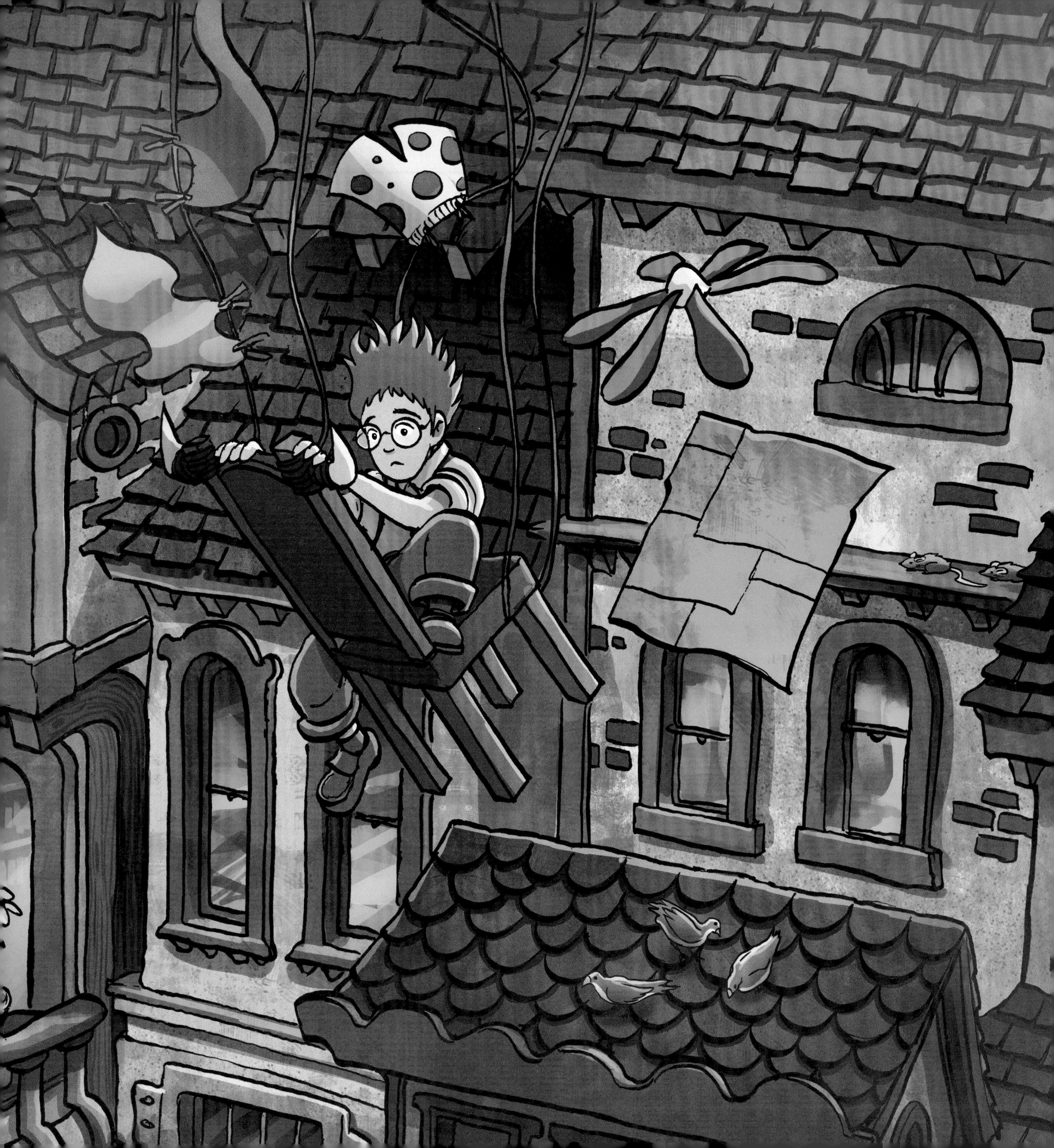

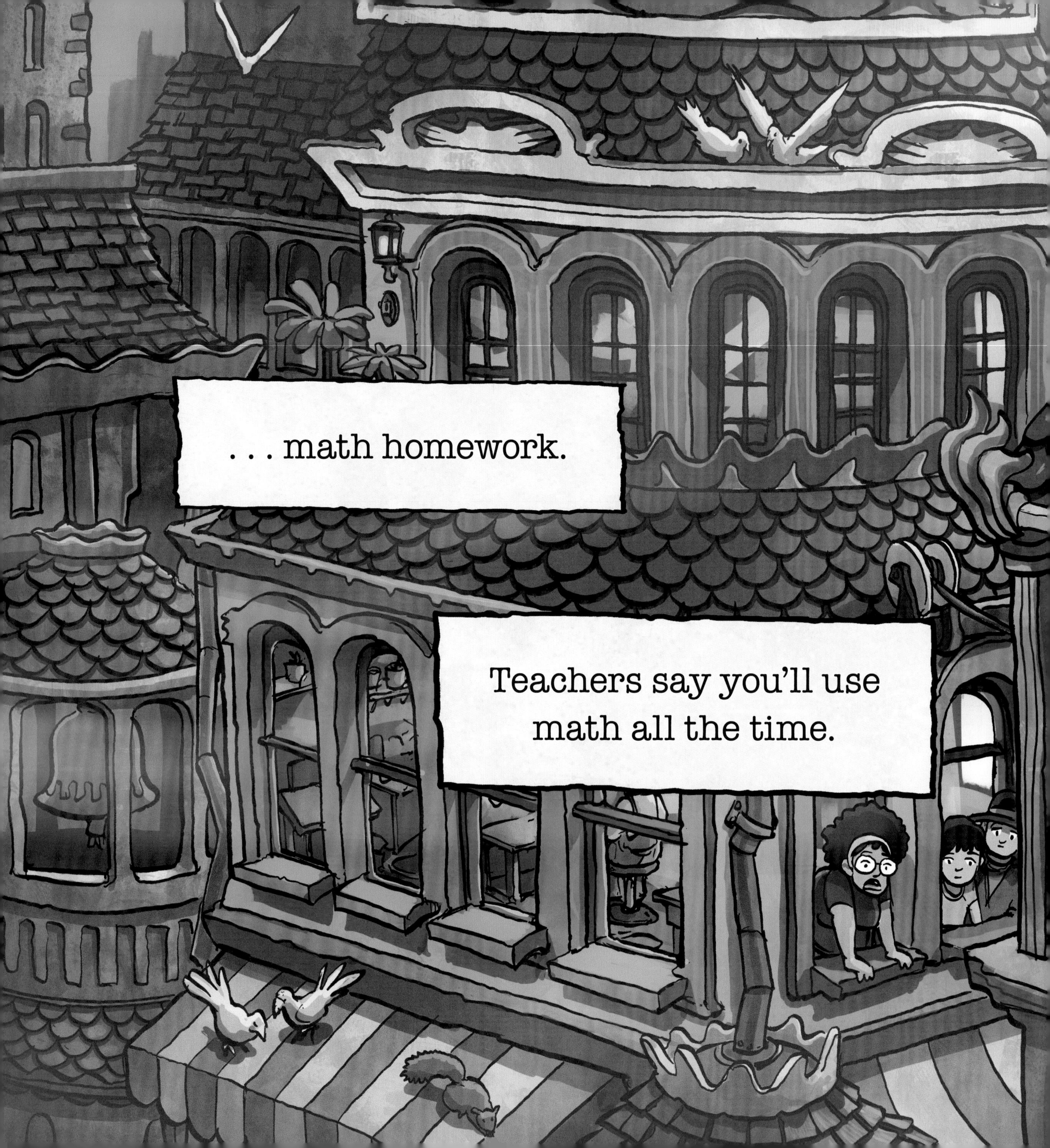
. . . math homework.
Teachers say you'll use math all the time.

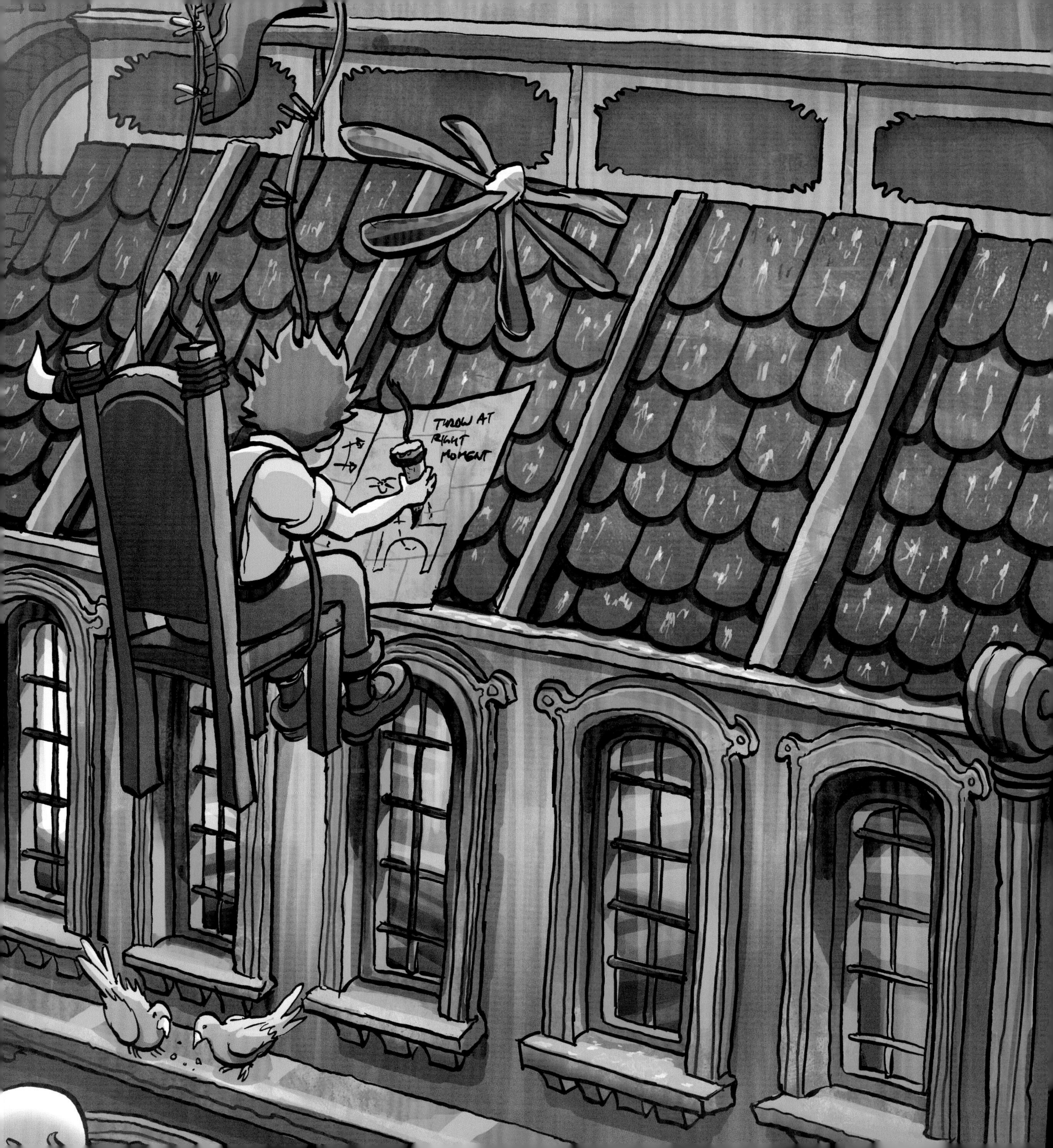
THROW AT RIGHT MOMENT

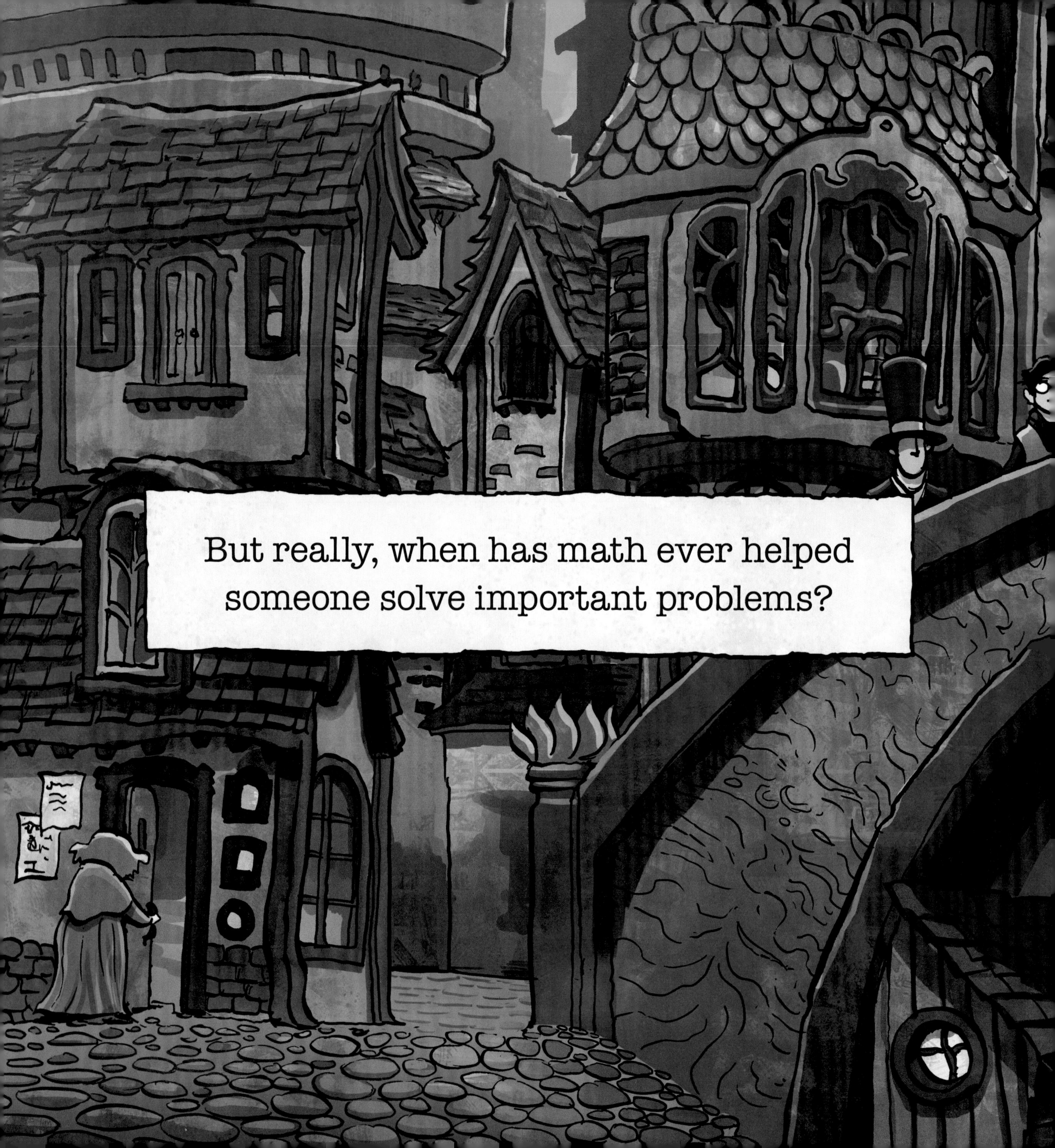
But really, when has math ever helped someone solve important problems?

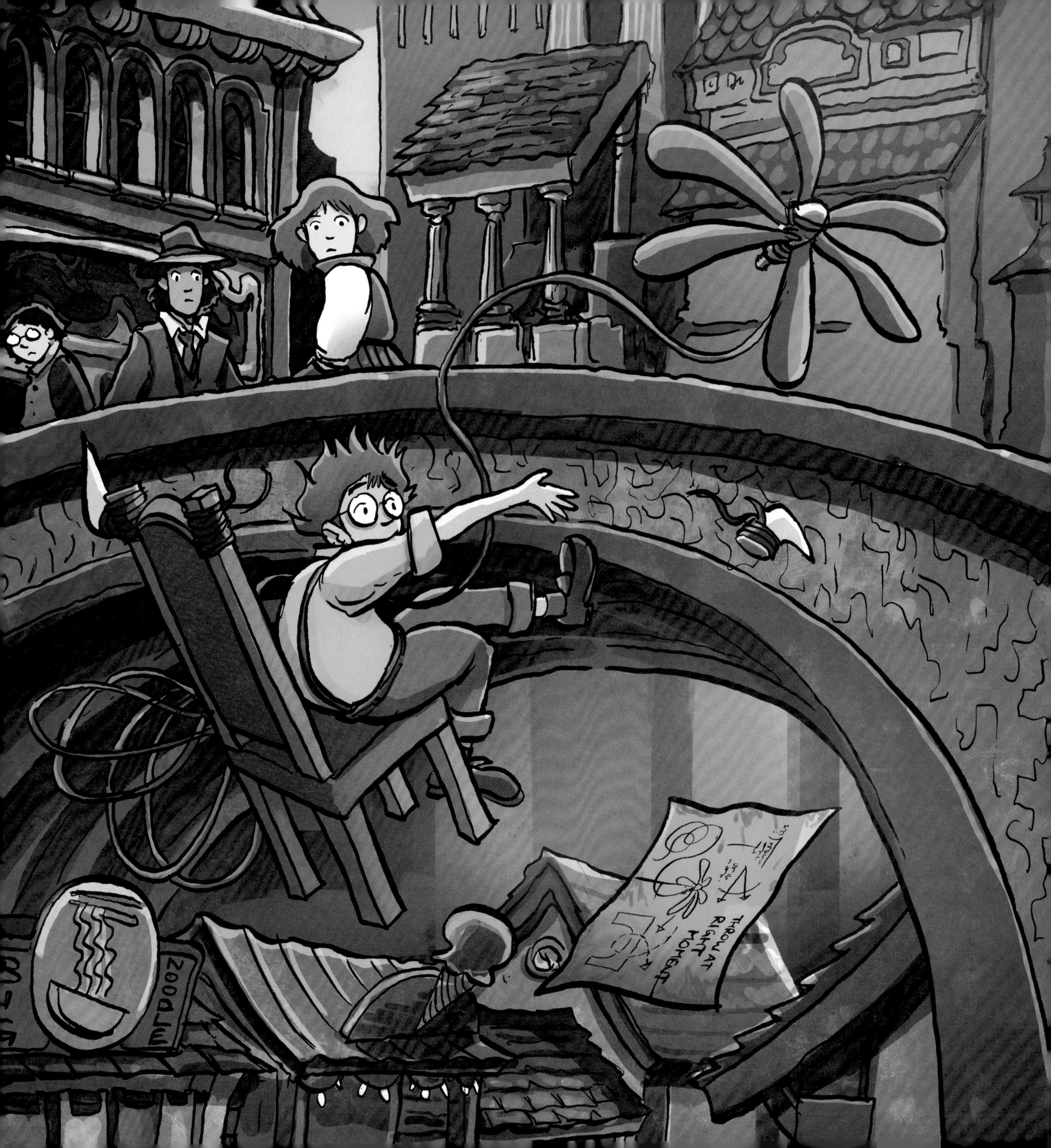
NOODLE
THROW AT RIGHT MOMENT

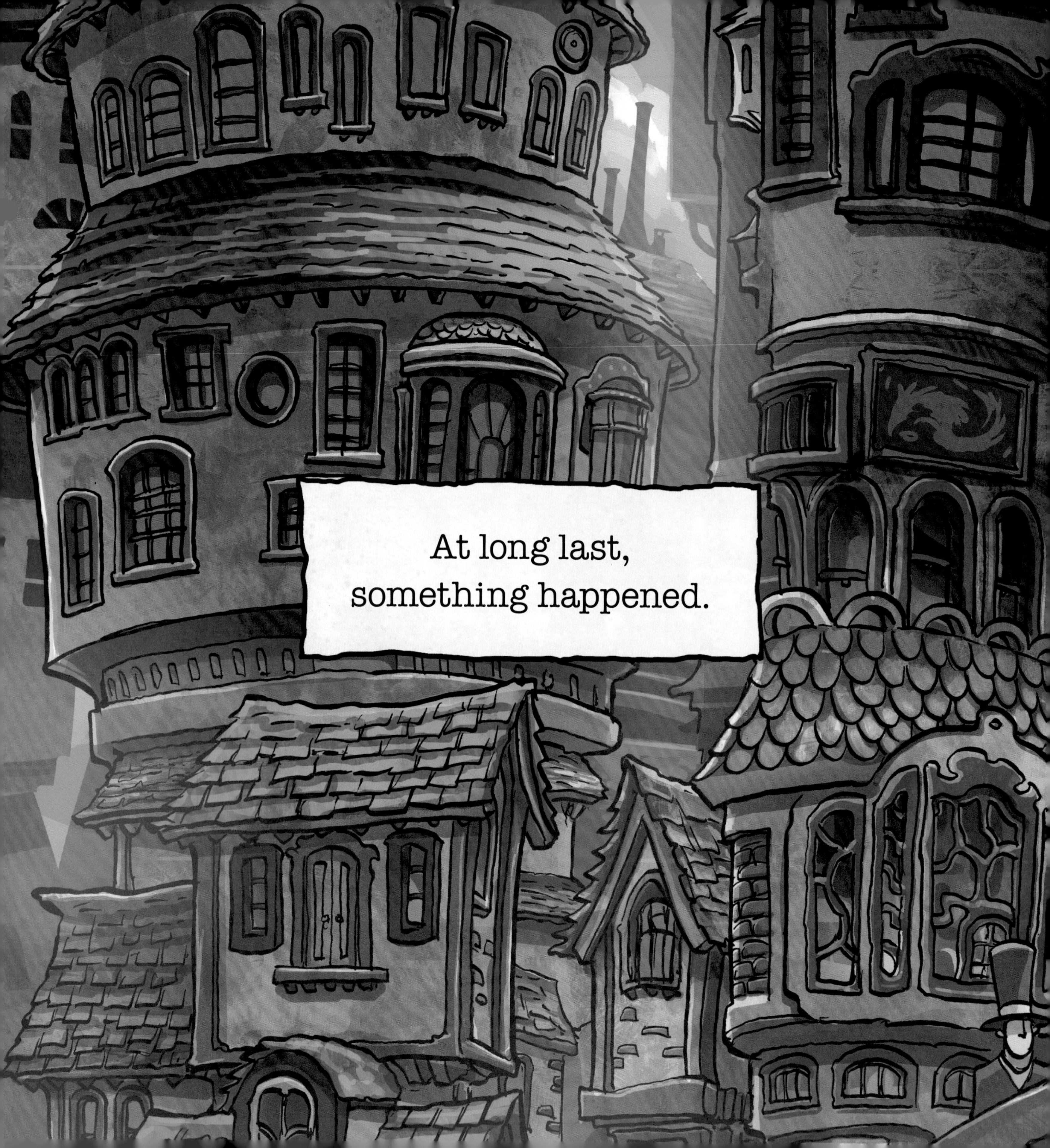

At long last,
something happened.

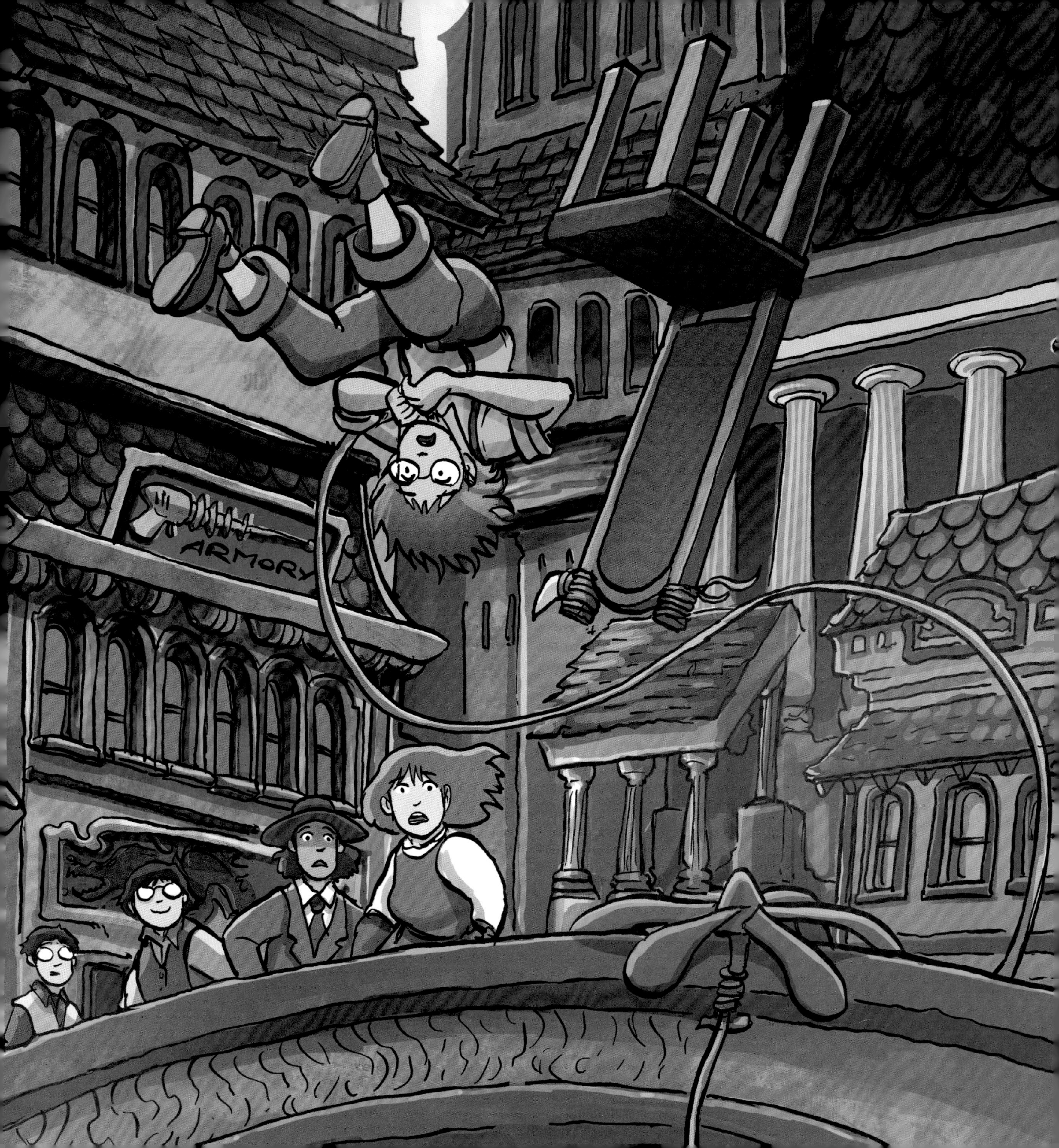
ARMORY

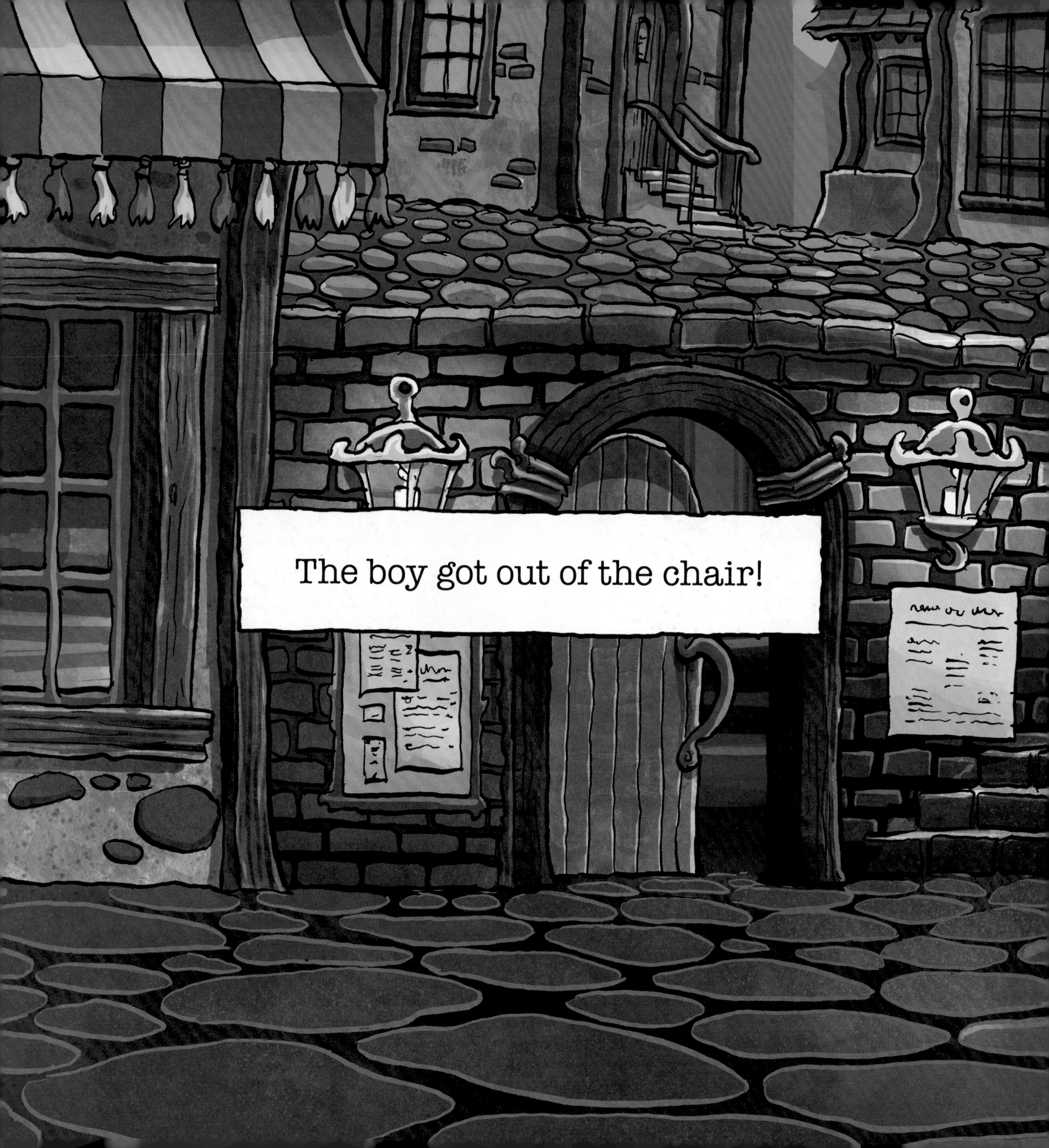

The boy got out of the chair!

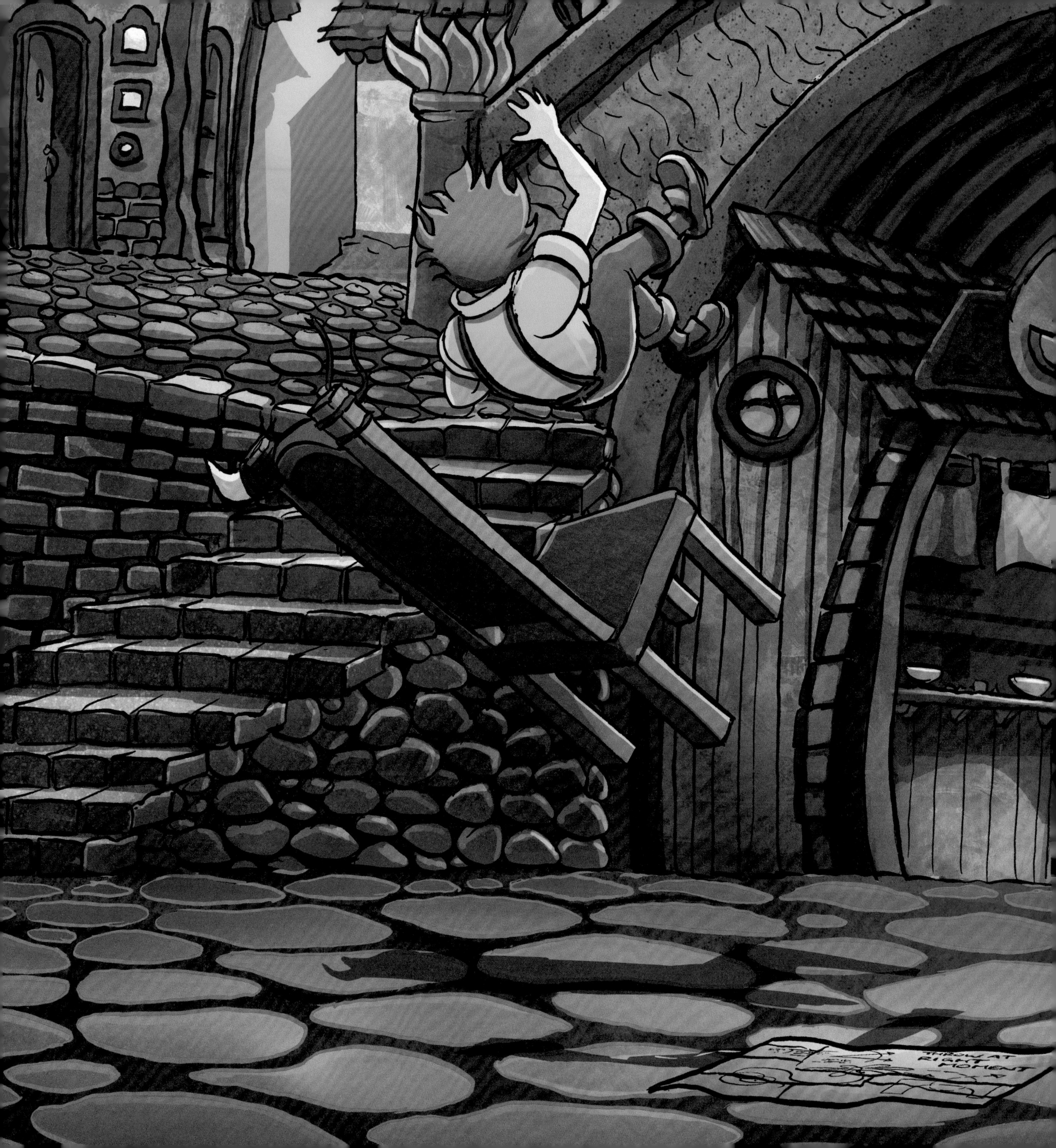
THROW AT
RIGHT
MOMENT

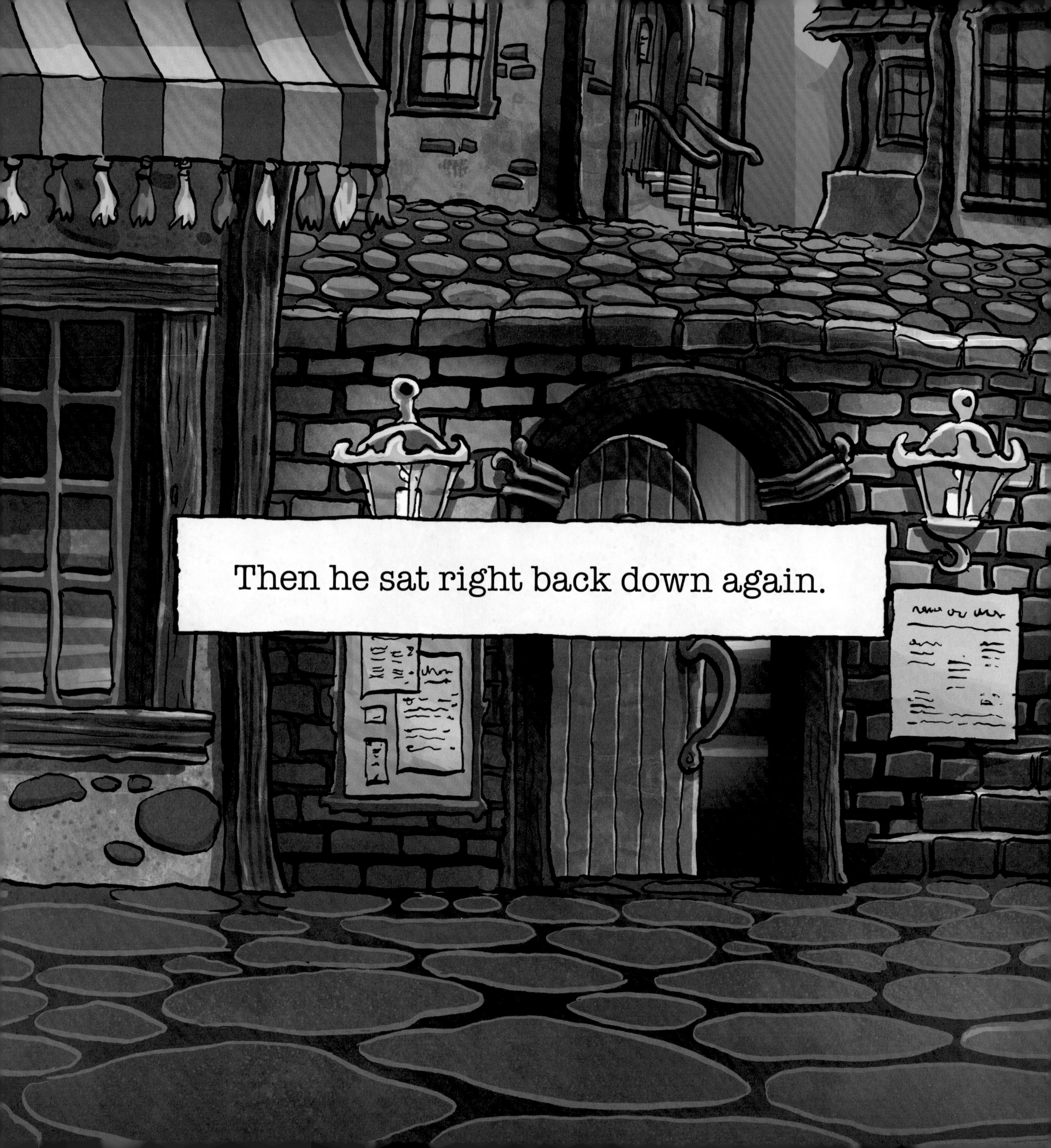
Then he sat right back down again.

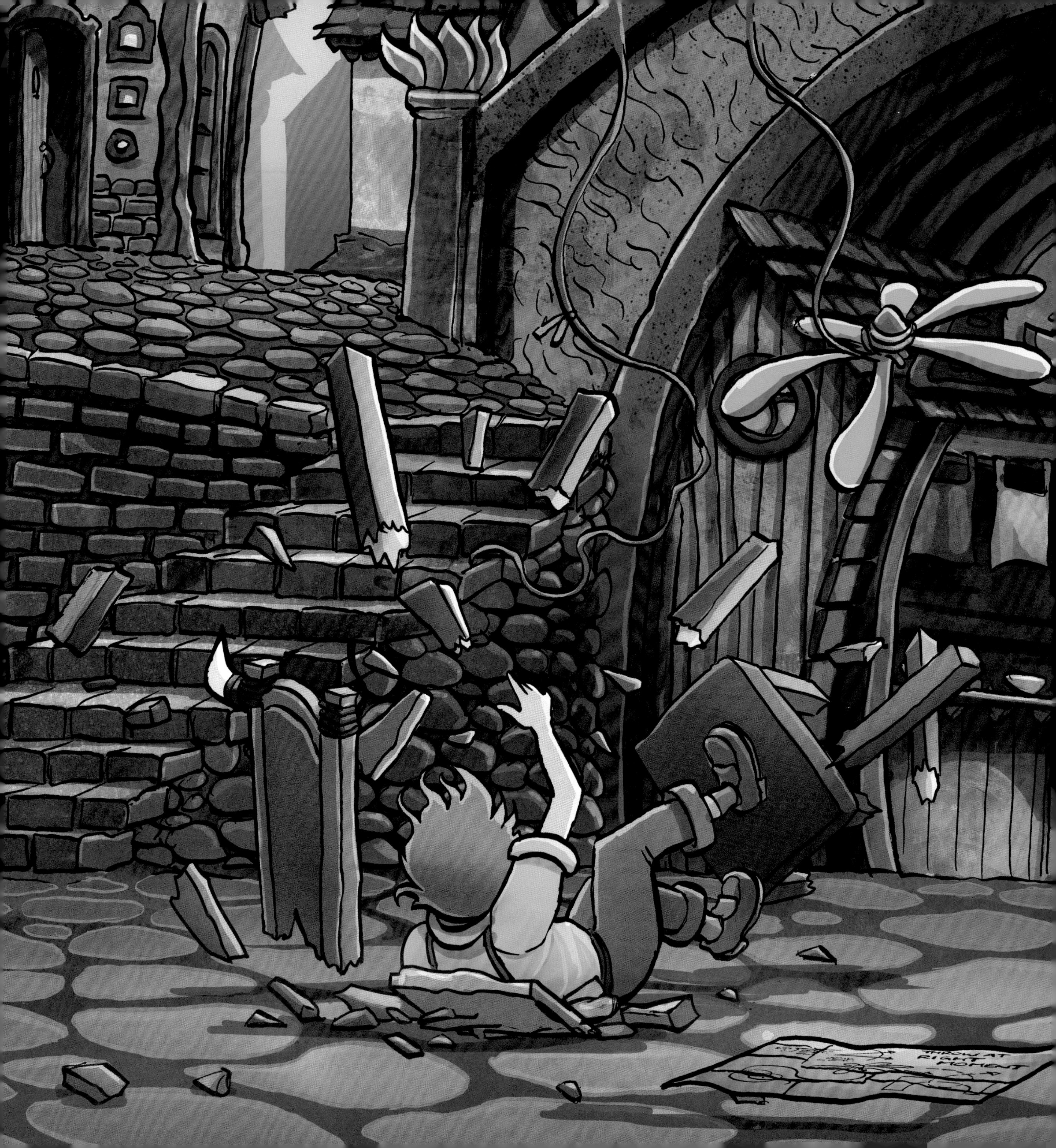
THROW AT RIGHT MOMENT

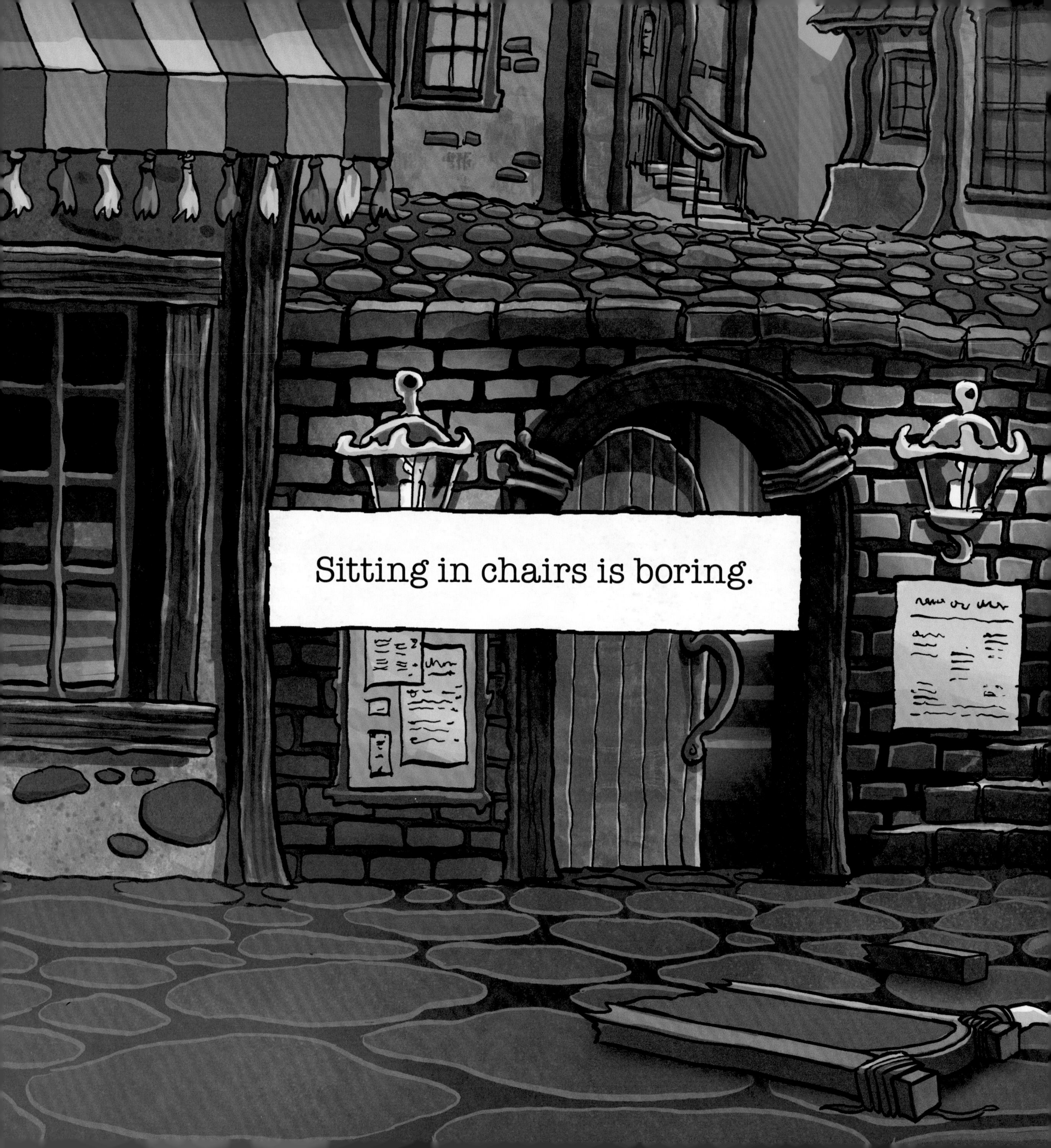
Sitting in chairs is boring.

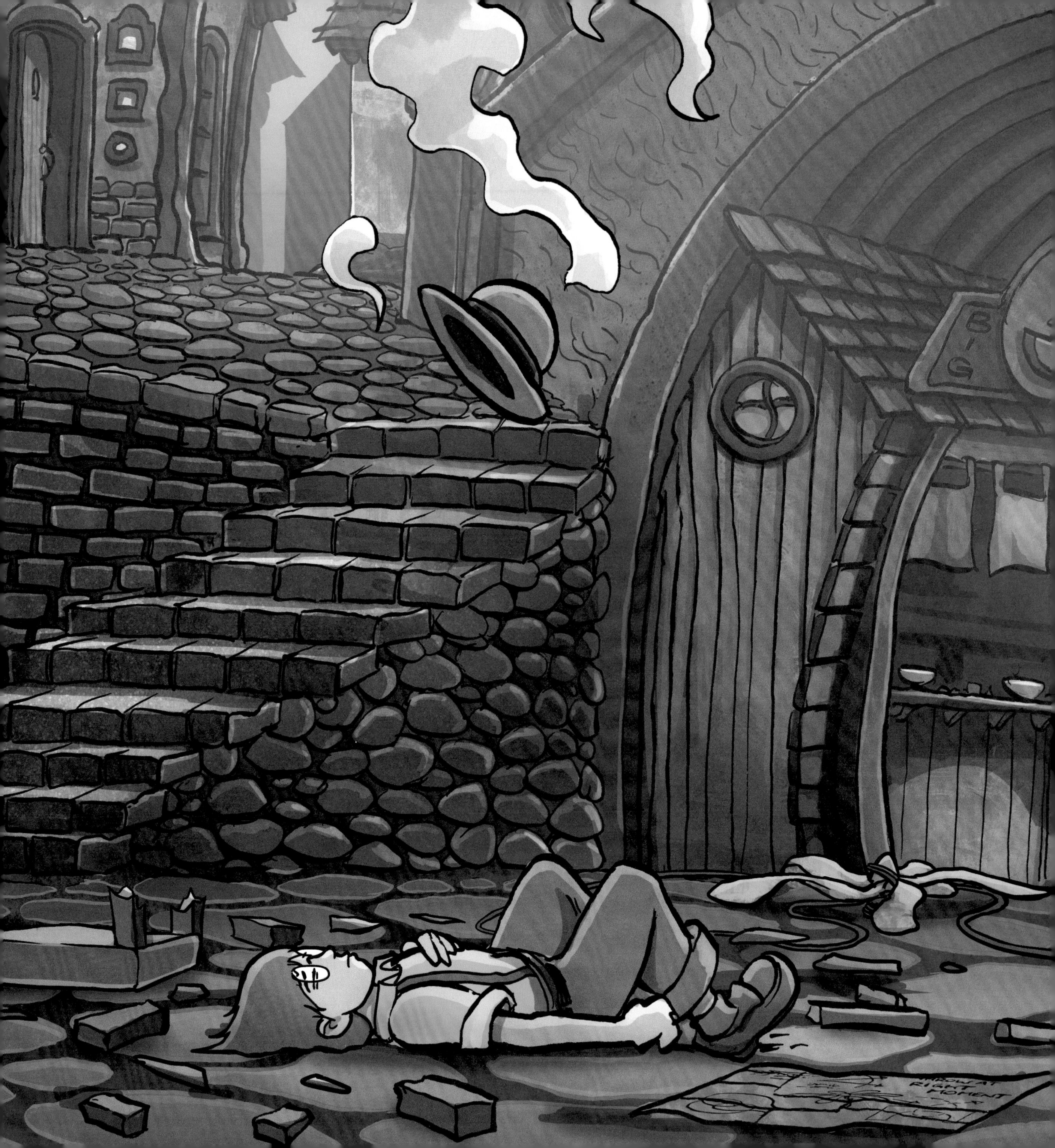
BIG
RIGHT MOMENT

The end.